FOGHORN PASSAGE

FOGHORN PASSAGE

ALISON LOHANS

Stoddart

AN IRWIN YOUNG ADULT BOOK

Published in 1992 by
Stoddart Publishing Co. Limited
34 Lesmill Road
Toronto, Canada
M3B 2T6

Canadian Cataloguing in Publication Data

Lohans, Alison, 1949-
Foghorn Passage

(Irwin young adult fiction)
ISBN 0-7737-5496-2

I. Title. II. Series.

PS8573.035F6 1992   jC813'.54   C91-095673-1
PZ7.L64Fo 1992

Cover Design: Brant Cowie/Art Plus Limited
Cover Illustration: David Craig
Typesetting: Tony Gordon Ltd.

Printed and bound in Canada

For my parents,
Walt and Mildred Lohans,
with much love

Acknowledgements

My sincere thanks go to the many friends who read and made helpful comments on this manuscript, but particularly to Stewart, Mary, Jill, and Rebecca and Mike.

One

*I*t was another raw November day, a Thursday afternoon. Wind and rain were lashing the entire B.C. coast, and on the bus between school and Youth Orchestra I'd glimpsed buoys tossing, startled orange flashes, in the swollen grey sea. The chilly gloom penetrated deep within me, a dampness that even a well-heated room couldn't dispel.

Orchestra practice was over now. Above the clatter of instrument cases and the snapping of latches, a loud silence buzzed in the rehearsal hall. Today Maestro Hoffmann had collected our music for the Beethoven violin concerto. In exchange, he'd given us a symphony. Now he stood at the podium talking to our new concert master, Geoff Harris-Hughes. Julie Blaustein was fuming about something as she put her violin away. In the back of the room, Leah softly went over a difficult passage on the tympani.

Amy Kesey was pestering Hilary and Renée and me to come to the hospital with her to see Matt.

Matt Bruckner, Amy's boyfriend, was a brilliant violinist, probably the best in the province. He'd been concert master, our principal violin, ever since I joined Youth Orchestra. When he performed, shivers tingled up my spine. Audiences loved him and stood, cheering, afterwards. Now he was paralyzed, victim of a car crash that had killed his sister and three others.

"He needs more visitors than just me. If you don't come he'll get the idea nobody cares." Amy's sweet face was reproving. Light shimmered off her waist-length dark hair.

I curled my fingers tighter around the handle of my French horn case and wished I could escape. It wasn't that I had anything against Matt, although sometimes he came across as arrogant, maybe even snotty. I hardly knew him. The real problem was Amy. She was asking too much, in a way that was calculated to make us feel guilty. To make it impossible to say no.

If the others wanted to go, fine. There was no reason I, Samantha Franklin, should get all guilted out. Plain and simple, I couldn't handle it. Not yet. Even if Matt was the genius some people said he was — at sixteen, my age, already playing first violin with the city symphony. Composing music. That had nothing to do with me.

Hilary Wong stood there leaning against her cello. "He must feel awful," she said, her sensitive face concerned. "So many terrible things happening."

"I sure wouldn't want it to happen to *me*," Renée blurted out. She chewed her lower lip.

I tucked my music folder under my arm and looked pointedly at the clock. "Mom expects me home by six."

"We won't stay long." Amy stared at the floor. "He's really depressed. Usually he makes me leave after only ten minutes."

"I'll come," Hilary offered, "if you think it'll help."

"Yeah, me too." Renée put her clarinet in her backpack and slipped into her jacket.

They were waiting. My cheeks went hot. I'd look like a jerk if I didn't go. It was easiest to pretend I'd planned to go all along. "If we're taking the bus, we'd better hurry," I mumbled. And then I closed my eyes, hating myself for being such a wimp.

Dusk was settling in. The wind whipped rain at my face as we stepped into the commotion of the Port Salish rush hour. Amy struggled with her umbrella, then gave up. I walked quickly, pretending the wetness didn't matter, pretending I wasn't scared silly.

Matt had it bad, all right. According to the newspaper, the other car went out of control when a deer ran onto the Semaphore Ridge Highway. After the impact that car flipped over a guardrail and burst into flames at the bottom of an embankment. I still got the shudders, recalling the front page photo showing Matt's crumpled Rabbit stranded like a crushed 7-Up can at the side of the road. Matt and the deer were the only survivors.

I squeezed my eyes shut. Images came too easily. Too vividly. It had been like that ever since . . . Without warning my toe caught on a crack in the sidewalk.

I blinked back to reality and breathed in the salty tang of wind blowing off the harbour; smells of rain on tarmac, exhaust. Several buses were coming. Hilary was out of breath from lugging her cello along at our fast clip.

There was standing room only. Amy's elbow jutted into my ribs and Renée's foot accidentally came down on mine. We lurched off balance as the bus started up. I grabbed Hilary's cello for support.

Amy's fingertips kept picking at the latches on her flute case. There was a hardness in her eyes that hadn't been there during orchestra.

I nudged her. "Do you go see him a lot?" I did feel sorry for her. It would be awful to have your boyfriend paralyzed.

Amy's damp hair jiggled in stringy clusters over her shoulders and down her back as she shook her head. "He acts like he never wants to see me." She glanced at me, almost furtively. "If he's not any different today with you guys along, I might not go back."

Something twisted inside me. Not go back? I didn't know Amy that well, and I certainly didn't know anything about her relationship with Matt. But how could she? Matt had a dead sister *and* a broken back. Either one was major bad news.

"Isn't this our stop?" Renée asked, reaching across a workman and his lunchpail to yank the bell cord.

I looked out at the hospital. The massive building sat there like a grim factory, a people-processor with multiple cycles. Birth. Pain. Illness. Death. It spat people out if they were all right, but some it gobbled down whole or bit by bit. I had too many memories of that place, memories Amy could never guess at.

There was no way I could go back. What was happening now had nothing to do with me, Sammie Franklin. I tried to squeeze out of the way, but I was wedged between Hilary's cello and Renée's shoulder, and a bunch of other people were trying to get off too. Our feet thunked down the metal steps. My French horn case bashed against the door.

The rain found my neck. I shrank into the warmth of my jacket and turned to Amy. "You're sure we won't be long?" Any excuse would do.

Amy shook her head and muttered something about Matt's not caring, not even if Beethoven walked into his room.

The fluorescent lighting. Disinfectant smells. Anxious visitors. The easy banter of hospital staff. It washed over me, an overwhelming tide. I hung back at the elevator. If my fingers got near the control panel they'd probably hit the button for the cancer ward. But there'd be a stranger in room 376.

"Has Matt got a TV?" Renée asked. "It must be pretty boring in here."

"All the rooms have TVs." There was a trace of disgust in Amy's voice. "But Matt won't even listen to his Walkman. And I bought him some new tapes."

We swept upwards with a sickening lurch.

I dawdled behind the others, pretending to read the numbers on the doors. 826. 827. 828 was a closet. Around a corner to 831, 832. Amy walked into 834.

It was a private room. A couple of cards sat on the bedside table. A poinsettia bloomed a cheery red on the window ledge. Behind it the drapes were pulled tightly. The person in bed had Matt's red-brown hair and lanky frame, but otherwise he was a total stranger. Matt Bruckner lay there like a sick old man.

My mouth went slack. It wasn't fair for Amy to drag me in to see this! There was the same emaciated face, with cheekbones jutting out in sharp points. The same deep sunken eyes. How could a person change so much in only three weeks?

"Hi," Amy said.

Matt looked at her. He looked at all of us with dull, tired eyes.

"How's it going?" Amy crept closer, but not close enough to touch him.

Matt muttered something while Amy stood there, stepping all over her own feet.

Renée giggled nervously and clutched her backpack in her arms. "How's the food in this joint?"

Amy turned. "He wouldn't know," she whispered. "He refuses to eat."

How *could* she? Matt wasn't deaf. I glared at her.

And then I was on the verge of tears. Too much of it was the same. The intravenous line dripping into Matt's arm. The catheter bag dangling from the bed rails. The wheelchair in the corner. The stack of blue plastic-coated pads in a visitor's chair. Incontinence pads. And there would be a plastic sheet in Matt's bed . . .

It had been exactly the same with Dad. And he'd died. Ten months ago. Of cancer. Paralyzed toward the end, after five years of impossible struggle. After a hospital stay that lasted from my grade nine year through the first half of grade ten. Including the summer in between.

I'd never forget that chilling day last January. In the waiting room. With my sister, Deena, and the ripped magazines. Jittery. Mom was with him. We knew he couldn't go on much longer. Then, the sound of running feet. The running feet that meant somebody was in deep trouble, the running feet that went down the hall as far as Dad's room and stopped . . .

"I have to go," I mumbled. "Hope things get better soon, Matt." I escaped down the hall and leaned on the elevator button, gulping in deep breaths so I wouldn't cry.

The others joined me soon afterwards. Amy's lower lip was wobbling. Hilary was looking at her brown cloth cello case. Renée was unnaturally quiet.

"He kicked me out!" Amy's voice came in little chunks of hurt. "What did I ever do to deserve that?"

"He's sick, Amy," Hilary said. Her soft oriental face was concerned. "When people get really sick sometimes they don't realize how much they can hurt people who care."

I winced. Dad. Feeling useless, lashing out at Mom, who kept right on taking it because she loved him, because he was dying. Dad. Taking it out on Deena and me, for being kids, for just being *there* sometimes. *I know all about it, Amy*, I thought. *Just ask me, I can tell you exactly how it feels.*

The elevator still hadn't come. Nervously I looked at Amy and wondered if I should say anything. She probably didn't know about Dad. After all, she went to E. L. Hendrie Senior Secondary, while I went to Tolliver.

I gave the elevator button another vicious jab and succumbed to the hurt in Amy's eyes. "He probably did it because you're still walking around," I said grimly. "And he'll never — " I swallowed hard. "He must feel guilty as hell about his sister, and good for nothing anymore. And wondering why you'd want a guy who's crip — " It was hard to keep going with a Styrofoam voice. I took a deep breath. "I bet he's hurting so much it hurts to care anymore." Heat roared into my cheeks.

There was a blank silence. I was afraid to look at them, especially Amy. But nobody said a thing, so I made one last try. "I know what it's like. My dad got like that. He was sick a long time, and he was paralyzed before it was all over."

"Oh, Sammie, I forgot." Hilary touched my shoulder. "This must be really hard for you."

Mutely I nodded.

But Amy hadn't been listening. "Well, I know how *I* feel too. He always treats me like garbage.

Why should I put up with that? Nobody's paying me. Let him rot in that bed. See if I care."

Hilary's eyes went deep with concern.

Renée looked embarrassed.

That kid could *die* if something didn't change. I almost blurted it out, but thought twice. What business was it of mine, anyhow? Why should I get all guilted out over Matt Bruckner? He and Dad weren't the same person. Matt didn't have cancer.

But there had been something in his face, in his eyes . . .

At last the elevator came.

Two

Supper was nothing to get excited about. Canned stew. Coleslaw. Toast. That was just as well, for I didn't have much appetite after the visit to the hospital.

Deena sat there, elbows propped on the table, talking with her mouth full. "I *hate* Ms. Barnett! Every time we have a test she acts like I'm gonna cheat. She sits there watching me like a witch, and then I can't concentrate."

"Maybe you're just imagining it," Mom said in a mild voice.

Deena's voice rose. "I'm *not*! She always watches me. And Karla, and Tyler Davies. One of these days I'm gonna stick a wad of gum in her marks book."

Mom sighed, but said nothing. Her face was lined in a way it never used to be. New grey streaks kept appearing in her wiry brown curls.

I played with my toast. "If she's as mean as you

say, she'd probably catch you in the act." Ms. Barnett was just a name to me. When I was in grade seven we still lived in our old house on Glencairn Road, and I'd gone to a different school. Now, in grade eleven, all that seemed such a long time ago.

"She would, too," Deena muttered. She ran her fingers through her dark frizzed hair and tipped her chair backwards. "Mom? Can I go to The Junction with Karla tonight? *Please*?"

Mom's face tensed. "I thought you had homework, Deena."

"Can't it wait? You don't expect me to study *all* the time, do you?"

I tuned out before the inevitable argument began. Deena and I weren't at all alike. I was too much the worrier. Broody, according to Mom. Deena was just the opposite. Sometimes Mom said she wished she could take the two of us and give us a couple of spins in the blender to even us out a little.

Matt Bruckner was haunting me. A coldness crept between my ribs as I remembered the look in his eyes.

The evening dragged on. Mom catching up on housework. Me studying, and Deena doing everything but, while all around us came the usual apartment noises. I hated apartment living, but we didn't have much choice. When Dad's disability payments ran out we'd rented our house to a couple of teachers with two little boys. Mom's cashiering job and the Canada Pension Plan cheques couldn't cover the mortgage, plus living expenses.

I sat there at the kitchen table doodling on my graph paper. In algebra we were learning quadratic equations. The long telephone cord stretched past me. Deena was sitting in the broom closet, door closed, talking and giggling.

"Deena!" Mom snapped as she walked in with a basket of clean clothes. "If you don't get off the phone this instant I'll have it disconnected. Believe me, if you want a life that's more than mopping floors, you'll have to get yourself through school."

There was a loud sigh behind the closet door. "I have to go," Deena said. "Talk to you later." She emerged wearing her winning smile. "I can't help it if Karla keeps calling me."

I put my head down on my math book. Deena had made the call herself, and Mom probably guessed as much.

Mom whacked the laundry onto the counter. "Look, Deena, if you bring home any more D's or F's, you'll be grounded with no phone privileges."

"I'll go do my socials report," Deena said in a hurry. But her dark eyes were lively as she whisked down the hall.

Mom took the telephone off the hook. "I'd appreciate it if you didn't say anything about this, Sammie," she said with a wry smile.

"No problem, Mom." No one would be calling me, anyhow, because Jen, my best friend, was spending the evening at her grandmother's. I drew the grid for another graph. The dripping tap was driving me batty. Our landlord wasn't the type who fixed things, not unless they were major.

So many things had changed. This cramped two-bedroom apartment was our second move. Here I couldn't even practise my horn without somebody complaining. Most of the dining room suite had been sold, and the piano too. I knew Mom missed the piano badly. But rent was high, and Dad hadn't been insured. Not that *any* amount of money could ever make up for his death.

Thinking about the changes made me feel like a selfish brat. What were a few things compared to Dad? Besides, Mom and Deena were hurting too. I knew Mom was discouraged with her job. A long time ago she'd taught kindergarten, and loved it. But these days few teaching positions were open. The sub list was full too. I knew that spending all day in a drugstore punching a cash register could never measure up.

And what about Matt Bruckner? Would he ever play violin again?

Unexpectedly, Mom's hand settled on my shoulder. "Is something bothering you, Sammie? You're awfully quiet."

I gave her a weak smile. "It's hard to concentrate." That was true, all right.

Mom patted my shoulder. "I think I'll have a shower, then read for a while. Don't stay up too late, dear."

I promised not to, and then wished I'd told her about the trip to the hospital. I needed to talk to somebody. I called Jennifer, but as the phone rang and rang I knew it might be a while before she got back from her Grandma Cascardi's.

Suddenly I felt incredibly alone.

Images of my father flickered like a video in front of my math. Dad, dark haired, dark eyed, smelling of shaving cream, on his way in his beige work clothes with "Bill" stitched in red above his pocket. Dad, relaxing in front of the TV, feet propped up on the coffee table. Dad, entertaining us at dinner with his boyhood escapades. Dad, his face worn with pain, suddenly old at the age of forty-three.

I almost walked out to the living room to look at the photo of him that sat on a shelf between Mom's poetry collection and some of her ceramic choir-boys.

Next door the Wallaces' TV blared. They were watching "L.A. Law." The people upstairs sounded like they were playing hockey in their living room.

My mind wandered. Matt's thin face. His long legs lying motionless beneath the covers. What on earth was the matter with Amy? Maybe I should talk to her. Except I'd feel pretty dumb trying to convince beautiful Amy Kesey that sometimes a person needs to give more than she's getting, to give, even though that other person is dishing out major you-know-what. Couldn't she see that, for Matt's sake?

It took me ten minutes to work through the next algebra problem. I tried calling Jen again. No answer.

Later the rain turned to fog. As the apartment quieted I heard the foghorns calling, like huge beings bellowing to one another across the harbour. A poem-feeling of anticipation tingled inside me. I loved the fog.

It was past eleven when I finally finished my assignment.

Deena was snoring with her mouth open. Her clock radio was still playing, her schoolwork scattered on the floor. How gross can a sister get? I shut off the music and crawled in bed.

Adam. Adam Hoover at school. Every night he filled my mind, bigger than life. But tonight he kept fading. So I listened to the foghorns. Sometimes Uncle Amos was out there on his fishboat, the *Ellen Marie*. I imagined the feel of mist on my cheeks, the air thick with the smell of low tide, in a ghostly world where spirits hovered just above the water. The air would tremble with the throbbing engines, with the chanting foghorns and clanging bell buoys; waves would slap against the hulls of boats at their moorings and . . .

"Huh?" Deena mumbled in her sleep. "Here, kitty kitty."

I went to the window and looked out over Port Salish. Downtown was shrouded in fog. Everywhere else lights mapped out the streets in neat rows, spilling into the hills. The hospital sat on Cordova Hill like a lit-up celebration. I stood there a long time. Looking, wondering, hurting.

"Shut up," Deena said irritably, and turned over.

I crawled back in bed.

Still I couldn't sleep as images came and went. Dad's cold body, wax-pale, lying in the hospital bed and staring with blank eyes at nothing. Matt, now a mere shadow of the guy who'd held crowds breathless with his playing.

At that moment I knew I was going back to the hospital. So what if I hardly knew Matt? He was a human being, and he was hurting. How could I live with myself if he were to give up, and I hadn't tried to help?

But after school the next day I put it off. I didn't even get around to telling Jennifer. That night I didn't sleep at all.

I was on my way to the bus stop by eleven on Saturday morning. My hands were wet with nervousness when I transferred at Fourteenth Avenue. I made myself not think, just watched buildings and trees emerge from the fog, watched fuzzy blobs of colour become traffic lights.

At the hospital the fog was cotton wisps dangling in blue. I wondered if Matt could see it, hear the foghorns. But probably he wouldn't care.

I almost didn't have the nerve to walk up the circle drive and in through the automatic doors. When the return bus pulled over across the street, I nearly made a run for it. Matt Bruckner didn't need me.

Inside, an elevator was waiting. I got in. When the doors opened to the cancer ward a hot sweat prickled over me. Sick, I jabbed eight and thankfully was moving again.

The bus might have been waiting for me. The elevator too. But Matt Bruckner sure wasn't.

He lay there, reddish hair uncombed, his face so

pale that his scattering of freckles looked like splotches of gold-brown paint. This time a tube was inserted in his nose, held in place by two pieces of tape. A bag of chalky liquid hung on an IV pole, dripping slowly into the nose tube. The sickly-sweet odour of concentrated food permeated the room.

"Hi, Matt," I said. It came out sounding scared.

"What're you doing here?" he asked in a pained voice. His eyes were brown, not the cold grey I'd always imagined from across the orchestra room.

I could see why Amy got upset. I was too nervous to even sit down. "I — felt bad about running out the other day." I gulped in a deep breath. "Having lunch, eh?"

For one whole minute he didn't answer. "Stupid tube feed," he finally muttered. "They shoved it down last night."

Silence rebounded off the walls. Every second it pulsated more loudly. I sat down in a chair full of incontinence pads. Hot shame instantly filled me, as if I were trying to hide the awful truth. Just a month ago Matt Bruckner had a lot to be proud of. Now he couldn't even control his bodily functions.

I had the uncanny feeling that he sensed my thoughts. "Why are they feeding you that way?" I blurted out. Not that I needed to ask. Dad had been on tube feed for a while. He'd quit eating too, after the paralysis set in.

A spasm of annoyance flashed in Matt's eyes.

I wrapped my feet around the chair legs. A

graceful exit was impossible. Matt had every right to wonder why I'd come. Until now I'd just been the girl in the French horn section. If he'd noticed me at all.

And then I saw the cast. Bulky and white, it showed through the neck of Matt's pyjamas, a ridge that went all the way across his chest and beneath his armpits. How could he *sleep* in the thing? I took a deep breath and asked him.

Matt's thin face twisted. "What's it to you?"

"Sorry," I mumbled. "That wasn't my business."

"Who gives a care, anyway," he said, swearing.

"We all do. I just thought — " Thought *what*, that I'd be able to cheer him up? What a laugh. "Everybody feels awful about what happened," I stammered. "But things'll get better. I bet you'll be back in orchestra in a few months."

He tried to move. All the poles attached to the bed frame rattled. All the tubes jiggled. But Matt didn't move much. He glared at me with hard glittering eyes. "They're paying a shrink to tell me all that crap," he said bitterly. "The social worker lays it on pretty thick too. Think I need to hear it from *you*?" He turned his head toward the closed drapes.

A moment later he started throwing up.

I handed him a basin and went to get a nurse. In the elevator I banged my head against the panelling until somebody else got in. How could I have been so *stupid*? Matt Bruckner didn't need my company. As I tried to shake off the humiliation, a faint satisfaction lapped at me. At least I'd tried.

Three

I didn't tell anybody about my second visit to the hospital, and forced thoughts of it to the back of my mind like an embarrassing secret. At school Jennifer and I watched Adam from a distance and I filled the margins of my notebooks with his name. But the whole thing came up again just before Christmas.

I was over at Glenna's to baby-sit Willie, and Jen had come along to keep me company. Afterwards she was going to sleep over.

Glenna was my half-sister. I'd hardly known her until I was nine. There had been a lot of tension between Dad and Glenna's mom, and after they got divorced, Glenna's mom took Glenna to live in Orca Sound for a while. The year they came back to Port Salish, Glenna had such a bad fight with her mom that she stayed with us for the whole summer. After that she was in and out a lot, even after she got married.

Glenna was getting ready to meet her husband, Greg, after work for a night on the town. She was gorgeous standing there in her slip, her skin a pale caramel colour, and her tummy slimming down again after being pregnant.

I glanced at my reflection in the mirror, next to hers. We looked like sisters. We both had the Franklin tawny skin tones, though mine was lighter, the same unruly dark hair. And there was something about our eyes, something that had come down the generations from our great-great-grandmother, daughter of a runaway American slave. I glanced at Willie, asleep in his crib. Willie looked more like Greg.

Glenna noticed me peeking at her baby and smiled. "I wish Dad could see the little guy. He'd be so proud."

"Did he ever see Willie?" Jennifer sounded self-conscious.

Glenna's face went sad, and I remembered her bulging belly at the funeral. Little Willie had been born three weeks later, named after a grandpa he'd never know. "No," she said.

For some reason I thought of Matt Bruckner, wondering if he was in the same bed, still hooked up to the tube feed. A kind of urgency caught me as I remembered his dull eyes. "There's this guy," I blurted out. "You know, the one from orchestra who was in that wreck? Some of us went to see him in hospital last month, and — "

"You never told me." Jen was surprised. "How come?"

I shook my head. "I forgot, I guess." I could hardly tell my best friend I'd kept something from her.

"Was he bad off?" Glenna asked.

"Paralyzed." I looked at my feet. "Not in danger anymore, I don't think, but . . ."

Glenna slithered into a slinky blouse. "That would sure put the screws to your life."

"Yeah. Especially if you were the one driving and your sister got killed. All because of a deer." The flowered bedspread was safer to look at. "It was like he'd given up. Like he was ready to die, like . . . And the way he plays the violin — " My throat knotted.

Jen glanced at me sympathetically.

"Poor kid," Glenna said. "How'd his family take it?"

I traced my finger around a large yellow bedspread flower. "How would I know? But his girlfriend sure can't handle it. She said she might not go see him again."

Jen was outraged. "*What*? How could anybody be so mean?"

Glenna paused with her makeup and caught my eye. "Sometimes things aren't so simple," she said.

I told them about my second visit. "I can see why Amy didn't want to go back," I said. "But there he is, all by himself. And he's not that kind of guy. I'd feel awful if he just — I mean, do you think he *could* do that? Die because there's nothing left to live for?"

"Whooo." Glenna sat there, mascara wand

poised. "Sounds like the kind who might try killing himself if the body does go and get well."

A malignant blackness churned around me.

Willie sat up in his crib and reached for Glenna.

"Shoot!" Glenna said. "I thought he'd sleep. This place is too small. Can't even breathe without waking the kid." But she smiled as she picked him up. "We need a bigger apartment, kiddo," she said, nose-to-nose with her baby. "Where you can have your *own* bedroom." She glanced at the clock radio. "And *I'm* going to be late." She deposited Willie in my arms. "Change him for me, will you, Sammie? I've got to run." She scowled at her reflection and yanked a skirt out of the closet.

I pushed back thoughts of Matt and grabbed a diaper. "C'mon Willie, you're soaked. Let's get you nice and dry, okay?"

Willie didn't agree. He twisted and yelled, trying to get free.

"He hates being changed these days," Glenna called. "Sometimes I practically have to sit on him."

I could see what she meant.

"This guy you were talking about," Jen said later. "How come you went to see him? I mean, you don't really *know* him."

I shrugged, though the gesture seemed a lie. "Because." Willie squirmed in my arms. I patted his back and set him on the floor with his bottle.

"Do you like him a little?" she persisted.

"Jen! Don't be gross." I could feel my face getting hot. Jen knew how I felt about Adam —

and how Adam felt about me, which was zip. "Why would I go visit somebody else's boyfriend? If I liked him, I mean."

Willie started dribbling his bottle onto the old carpet. Glad for the diversion, I jumped to stop him. "Willie! No-no. We don't do that." I opened a magazine. "See the nice picture, Willie?" But the glossy advertisement in Glenna's *Chatelaine* didn't appeal to him. With an ear-shattering shriek he crawled toward the small Christmas tree, which was strategically placed between a ratty old stuffed chair and a stereo speaker.

Jennifer grinned. "Can't win, huh?"

I turned on the TV, but Willie wouldn't stay still. For a while we all went crazy crawling around chasing each other. At last he dozed off in my lap.

In the sudden quiet I looked down at my nephew, cheeks still flushed and his curly fair hair tinged with sweat. A foghorn boomed, startling me. Willie stirred but didn't wake. The sound was so much louder at Glenna's place, in the Harbour District. Outside a streetlight cast a cottony glow in the fog.

Jennifer switched the TV channel. *Cabaret* was showing on CTV. "We should make some popcorn," she said.

But the door rattled and Glenna and Greg bounced in, all smiling and relaxed. Willie woke up and wanted to nurse.

Greg turned to me. Although he was twenty-three, Glenna's age, he still had a skinny half-finished look about him. "We were talking about your friend in the hospital," he began.

My *friend*? That was stretching it a bit. "Yeah?" I said cautiously.

"It's that time of year when everybody wants to be home."

I groaned inwardly. Greg was using his insurance-salesman voice. As it was, this would be our first Christmas without Dad. Greg knew that, so what was he getting at?

"We were talking about how Christmas is at the hospital," Glenna explained. "What if you rounded up a bunch of people, grabbed a couple of pizzas and came in with a boom box and some good tapes? Throw a little party."

I looked at her suspiciously. "I hardly know him."

"It might help, kiddo." Glenna looked at her baby, away from my glare. Willie put his small hand possessively on her breast.

"I'll think about it." My voice was flat. Me, organize a party for Matt Bruckner? I didn't even know what type of music he'd want. And if Amy took it wrong, she'd never speak to me again.

Jen and I were quiet all the way home. I had the uncomfortable feeling she was thinking Glenna and Greg were *too much*.

Once home, I wished we could go right back to Glenna's. Aunt Vivian was over. And my imbecile jerk of a cousin, Blake.

The minute we stepped inside, Aunt Vivian cornered me with all kinds of dumb questions about school. I shot Jen my groan look. Aunt Vivian was Mom's sister-in-law, married to Uncle Amos. She could be a real pain. And Blake, at fifteen, was more of a slimy scum than a relative — the kind who'd fit in real well in the back alley. To make matters worse, Deena was strutting around with her developing bustline held proudly out for Blake's benefit.

We had to sit and be polite for thirty agonizing minutes. When Blake started sending Jennifer *looks* it became absolutely unreal. As Jen squirmed beside me, I plotted devious ways of exploding the enormous pimple on Blake's nose. With Aunt Vivian running the show like a friendly pit bull, excusing ourselves was out of the question. That woman thought she could boss *everyone*. She even had the nerve to tell Mom she ought to raise the rent for the Townsends, the family living in our house.

At last Aunt Vivian stood up, worrying about her poor Amos who was out on his boat overnight, and whether she and Blake would be able to get across town in the fog.

I just about took a fit laughing. Uncle Amos probably felt more at home on his boat than he did in his own house — after all, look who else lived there!

I'd swear Jen read my mind, for her elbow jabbed into my ribs and all of a sudden she was jiggling suspiciously. I didn't dare look at her. Then Blake gave her another *look*, as if he were the sexiest thing around. In spite of his amazing acne.

It was too much. I sputtered. Jen stood up, her face a mottled pink. Deena smugly straightened her shoulders to display her front. Across the room

Mom had something of a twinkle in her eyes as Jen and I escaped.

We had to half smother ourselves with pillows so they wouldn't hear us laughing. When the front door closed at last we howled, rolling on the beds until our stomachs hurt.

Deena walked in. "What's so funny?" she asked.

Jen landed flat on her back on the floor. "Can you *believe* it?"

"True love," I choked, clutching my stomach. "Oh Jen, at last you've found him. What will your mother say?"

"What's with you guys?" Deena persisted. "Have you gone mental or something?" She turned on her radio.

"Out!" I pointed with my thumb.

"You can't kick me out of my own room!"

Rather than wreck things by arguing, I flung my pillow at Jen. She hurled it back, right at my face, while Deena stood there watching.

"You can have the room in ten minutes," I said. "Go take a shower or something."

Sullenly Deena grabbed her nightgown and left.

Jen giggled harder. "How'd you ever get a cousin like *that*?"

I rolled my eyes and pretended to throw up. "You'll have to ask Aunt Vivian. At least it's not catching — I *think*."

Jen fell to her knees, extending her arms. "Oh, Blakie — *Blakie*!" she wailed. "Wherefore art thou, my own dearest love?"

I bit my pillow to keep from exploding. "Down

in the gutter, dearest," I gasped once I could talk again. "Slurping up the slime, yum yum!"

"Oh — *gross*!"

There was a loud thumping in the floor.

Right away Jen clapped her hands to her mouth. "Uh-oh. I forgot this was an apartment."

"I hate it," I muttered. I was tempted to stomp around the room a few times, or maybe rearrange the furniture.

Jen went silent.

I changed into my nightgown, trying to swallow the sudden resentment, and knocked against the wall adjoining the bathroom. "Hurry up, Deena!"

"Are you going to do what Glenna suggested?" Jen asked later as we lay in sleeping bags on the living room floor. "Throw a party for this Matt guy?"

I shook my head. "Are you kidding? Nobody'd listen to *me* — except Hilary and Renée, maybe. And it would take more than just us to make a party happen."

"Yeah." Jen propped her chin in her hands. "Poor guy, though." She paused. "What's he look like?"

The question took me aback. "Kinda tall," I said. "Kinda thin. Sort of red hair, brown eyes — not exactly good looking, but, well, intense. Remember, I don't know the guy. But the way he plays the violin, well . . ."

There was no way I could tell her how Matt's music made me feel. Like a bird soaring on currents of air, like seeing into another dimension where sounds had colours and shapes, maybe even flavours. Like the rest of the world had disappeared, leaving only me and the music.

"So he's really good, eh?" Jen said quietly. "Have you got a picture of him?"

Actually, I did. Last May a photographer had taken pictures when we played at the Canada West Festival, and I'd bought a print. I tiptoed into the bedroom and tried not to wake Deena as I sorted through my scrapbooks.

"Here," I said, pointing him out to Jen.

She studied the photograph for a minute or two, then handed it back. I scooted closer to the light and looked at it. There I was, fourth horn, kind of hard to see behind Ian McCall's bassoon. There was good old Renée with her clarinet, and Hilary in the middle of the cellos. Julie Blaustein looked really sharp in her old position right behind Matt in the first violin section. And there was Matt, sitting straight and proud.

Something crumpled inside me and sudden moisture filled my eyes. Even if he did make it back to orchestra, Matt Bruckner would never, ever sit that way again. I gulped in a deep breath, hoping Jen wouldn't notice the tears. "When that guy plays a solo the concert hall goes absolutely *silent*," I said. "It's just him standing there in the spotlight, with blackness beyond — and the music. It gives you shivers."

"No wonder he's so depressed," Jen murmured.

I sighed. "He must really *feel* things to play like that. He — "

"Like his girlfriend?" Jen interrupted with a

wicked grin. "Are you *sure* you don't like him, just a little?"

I gaped at her sudden change of gears. The weepy feeling was instantly gone. I whomped her with my pillow instead.

Four

I forgot about Greg and Glenna's idea. But as it turned out, a week and a half later twelve of us from orchestra showed up at the hospital with our instruments. When Maestro Hoffmann announced that he wanted people to sign up to play carols at the hospital, the other three horn players — Troy, Jason and Arthur — promptly came down with malaria or something. So guess who got elected. Amy did not come.

It was right after supper, the time when the most visitors always came. We drew curious looks as we lugged our instruments through the automatic doors. Maestro, slim and elegant in his suit and red tie, didn't seem to notice.

"I hope they have a decent chair for me," Hilary whispered. "Or I'm out of luck."

I could try that excuse. Being concerned about Matt Bruckner was one thing. Actually facing him after my disastrous solo visit was something entirely different. My palms were sweating and my heart thudded in my ears.

Maestro, of course, had everything meticulously organized. Twelve chairs and music stands awaited in the patients' lounge on Matt's floor.

We warmed up and tuned. In some ways it wasn't much different from an ordinary performance — except this time our audience wouldn't be dressed in furs and suits.

Renée turned to me. "I hope Matt's doing better," she said.

"Yeah." Nervously I fluttered my fingers on the flat keys of my horn, and tried to keep my face averted as patients began arriving. Furtively I glanced at them. Wheelchairs. IVs. One woman had even been wheeled in on her bed. Other patients had no apparent disability.

Matt wasn't in the crowd. Sounds of a not-so-muffled argument came from a room down the hall, though. At least one voice wasn't muffled, and it was a voice we all knew. Maestro seemed impervious to the foul words that scattered amongst us like pellets of rat poison. He tapped his baton against his stand and claimed our attention.

We played and lingered for refreshments. A few kids went to say hi to Matt. Hovering in our midst was a kind of collective embarrassment.

"It makes sense for him to feel that way," Renée whispered at my side. "But it sure doesn't make him look good."

Hilary traced her finger around the rim of her plastic cup. "I'm glad Amy didn't come," she said at last.

I sipped my hot cider and wished I went to E. L. Hendrie Senior Secondary too, so I could keep up on the gossip. "She's still visiting him?"

"Just barely," Renée said. "She's sure giving other guys the eye, if you know what I mean."

The news left me feeling hollow. "Doesn't she care?"

Both Hilary and Renée were silent. And that told me clearer than words what they thought.

A violin bow darted into our midst. "Ladies!" Julie Blaustein said briskly. "We have been invited to play at the psychiatric unit. Just in case you wanted to be informed, before His Holy Highness decides to assert his so-called authority."

I had to grin. Everybody knew Julie was not fond of Geoff Harris-Hughes, the stuffy self-important snob who'd taken over as principal violin. A second performance was fine with me. Anything to get away from Matt's depressing ward. "The psych unit's on the fourth floor," I said. "Want to go on down and leave the guys to carry all the music stands?"

Julie's green eyes gleamed. "Lead on, milady!" She turned, knocking over a stand. The clatter shot a hush through the soft rumble of voices. Julie quickly righted it, but I couldn't help staring. One thing Julie Blaustein was *not* was a klutz. Classy, yes. Cool, yes, the type who stayed on top of any occasion. An instant later she was beckoning for us to follow her.

With straight faces we told Maestro where we were going. Then we scuttled to the elevator and didn't dare laugh until the doors shut behind us. Relief flooded through me. It was followed instantly by guilt. Who in their right mind *wouldn't* go into a slump if they were sentenced to life without the use of half their body? Matt's reaction hadn't been all that different from Dad's, at first.

It was snowing when we left the hospital, wet sloppy snow that splatted onto the sidewalk. Julie flashed a set of keys and offered Hilary, Renée and me a ride home. The Volvo was roomy, but even so Hilary and I were squished with her cello for company in the back seat. As the car skimmed down the wet streets, radio booming and Christmas lights glowing everywhere, things began seeming really all right. Before I knew it, I was asking if they wanted to go for a Coke.

"Chips!" said Julie. "With vinegar."

"What about our instruments?" Hilary asked. "Will they be all right in the car?"

"No prob." Julie honked at a bus that pulled out in front of us. "I'll park by the window. A cello's hardly something you can stuff in your pocket for a quick getaway."

Renée giggled.

A giddy recklessness danced inside me as Julie made a sharp U-turn at the intersection of Qualicum and Eighth. "We'll look for sweeties on the way," she announced, grinning over her shoulder at Hilary and me. The car shot forward with a squeal of tires. "My *mothah*," Julie went on, carefully enunciating each syllable, "would take a *hairy spazz* if she saw me right now. 'Young laedies must ahlways be awah of theah appearance in public.' Preserving the ladylike image. What rot. So she sends me to ye olde Manchester Oaks Academy, 'the superiah centah of leahning foah cultuahed young laedies.'"

Renée giggled harder. "See any sweeties, anyone?"

"There!" I pointed to a white car that was somewhat ahead in the next lane. Actually, I wasn't sure, but we were just having a good time, so what did it matter?

Julie gunned the engine and pulled abreast of the other car. We all waved.

It was two old ladies. The driver sat straight and prim, concentrating on her driving, but the other woman saw us and waved back with a wide lipsticked grin.

Julie cleared her throat. "Sammie. When I used the term 'sweeties,' I was thinking of someone other than sweet *grannies*. They're sweet, I'm sure, but what I had in mind were members of the opposite sex, you know? And rather younger than these two?"

Still waving, I fell back laughing as Julie pulled into the parking lot.

The Junction was nearly empty. As we stepped up to order, two girls rushed to wait on us while the manager lurked in the background. We had no problem finding a table by the window. By the time our order was ready, Julie's windshield was covered with soft snow. An overhead speaker blatted out gross Christmas music, the kind they play in stores to make you buy more.

Renée giggled. "We should get our instruments."

Hilary's eyes sparkled as she sipped her Coke. "We could show them the real thing."

"The real thing," Julie mused. "Who knows The Real Thing? We go about in a celluloid drama, scarcely knowing what comes from the computer of a paid script-writer and what's been with *person*kind since the days of yore. The shame of it!" She broke off with a dry smile. "Don't mind me, ladies. Sometimes I get carried away." She popped several chips in her mouth, sighed, then meticulously licked her fingers.

I slumped back, relaxed. My chocolate-dip cone was melting fast, so I couldn't do much talking.

Renée took a large mouthful of her loaded burger. "Ummm. This sure beats sitting at home. 'No, you can't watch television, Renée, your father's watching a special program. Turn down your radio, dear, it rather wrecks the atmosphere.'"

"Aye aye, sir!" Julie gave a mock salute. "What a world this is. Can't stay out late. Can't throw the odd party. Have to wear those dis*gus*ting *un*iforms to school."

"Can't pig out," Renée added. "'I wish you'd lose ten or fifteen pounds, dear. You'd look so much more attractive.' Can't smoke, drink, swear, do drugs." She giggled self-consciously. "Not that I'd *want* to do that."

"'You mustn't *do it*, dahling,'" Julie said in mincing tones. "'So many young men are *unclean*, if you follow me. There is such a risk of *disease*. (Sniff, sniff.) At any rate, we wouldn't want our Juliet to end up *pregnant*, now would we?' Hah!" Julie slapped the tabletop. "I ought to give *them* that lecture. No telling what *they'll* bring home one of these days. I hope she gets AIDS."

Shocked, I glanced at Hilary. She was terribly quiet. But then a glint darted through her dark eyes. "Can't sleep in. Can't sleep out. Can't sleep — "

"At all!" I sputtered, laughing. Little did they know.

"Can't practise," Renée said. "'It makes so much noise, dear. You mustn't forget your father's migraines. Can't you do it when he's at work? Better yet, why not practise at school?'"

"Amen!" I said. Without warning, tension clamped over me. "I *can't* practise." And I told them about the thin walls in our apartment building. About how I'd even tried practising in the storage room and the laundry room, and almost every time somebody complained. I didn't mention the way my lip muscles were losing their strength. Maestro couldn't tolerate weak players.

"You should send the manager a bill," Julie said. "For upgrading culture on the premises."

"Or give lessons to all the kids in the building," Renée added, laughing.

I sat there looking at the three of them. They lived in other parts of town. Went to rich schools. Could they even guess what it was like?

The face of my watch caught the reflection of the fluorescent tubes overhead. Somehow it was already ten-thirty. I wiped my mouth and reluctantly said I had to get home.

We had carefully avoided talking about Matt.

Five

*C*hristmas came a few days later. When I awoke that morning, my first impression was of light There was a catch in my throat at the thought of Dad and how we'd have to get through the day without him, but the brightness beyond the curtains was too compelling.

I draped myself in my comforter and crept past my snoring sister to the window. Whiteness was everywhere, topping the neighboring apartment buildings, caught in the spindly staked trees. The rising sun glanced off it, a startling newness bathing the city and surrounding hills. From below came the sound of clanking chains as a car navigated the snowy street.

I shook Deena awake. "Deena! It's Christmas."

For a moment my sister was soft-eyed with sleep. "Huh?" Then she sat up straight and pushed her frizzy hair back from her face. She bounced out of bed and yanked the curtains open. "It snowed again! Now it even *looks* like Christmas!"

Our eyes met. "Do you think Mom . . . ?"

We both listened. The shower was running in the Wallaces' apartment next door. Farther down the hall I could hear little kids screeching and laughing. So far there'd been no sound from Mom's room. Was she lying there awake, or simply sleeping?

"Let's make breakfast," I whispered. "We can surprise Mom."

Deena's face lit up. "Good idea. But first, I'm making a snow angel." She pulled on her neon pink jogging suit over her pyjamas. Together we tiptoed into the living room.

Our small tree had several new presents beneath it. When I plugged in the lights, red and gold danced off tinsel; near the fawn we hung every year, blue sparkled from one of the old silver balls. A kind of magic hovered in the air.

Deena tapped my shoulder. "Look, Sammie. The stockings. We shoulda made Mom hang one too."

At Mom's insistence we'd hung them from the bookshelves. Now a frosted gingerbread girl and cheery candy cane peered from each one, and odd shapes lurked below.

A lump swelled in my throat. It was too late to fix a stocking for Mom. Any strange sounds, and she'd be out to investigate.

I poured water into the coffeemaker, scooped the aromatic dark grind into a filter.

"Be back in a couple minutes," Deena said in a subdued voice.

She returned with cheeks and nose pink, tiny clumps of snow clinging to her dark hair. By that time I had bacon spitting in the skillet. Deena's eyes glowed as she held out a pine branch with two perfect small cones, and a delicate crystal bird. "See what I found! Somebody musta dropped it. It was there in the snow by the bus stop bench."

I cupped my hand around the bird. Fishing line ran through a hole in its back. I held it up to the window.

"Oooh!" Deena gasped.

Speckles of rainbow colours danced across the table, across the stove and fridge. "Oh Deena!" I gathered her into a tight hug. "Mom'll love it."

Mom's eyes misted when we carried the tray into her room. Then she smiled. "Why don't you bring your breakfasts in too. It'll be nice and cozy that way."

Deena lingered to show Mom the crystal bird, but I didn't mind. More than anything, it was important to make it through the day without getting depressed. Since Aunt Vivian and Uncle Amos had invited us for Christmas dinner, I felt like guarding every bit of time that belonged just to *us*.

Deena's voice was hushed as I returned balancing plates and juice glasses. "I remember, he'd lift me right up so my nose would touch the star on top of the tree."

They were talking about Dad. I set everything down and looked at the image smiling at us from

Mom's dresser. In that particular photo Dad's dark eyes glinted with a happy secret. But then, uninvited, a whole swarm of unhappy memories buzzed like wasps around me, transforming the familiar face into a smiling stranger.

Last Christmas we'd carried everything into his hospital room, even a little tree. He'd been cranky and more or less tolerated our being there, until suddenly he buzzed for a pain shot right in the middle of opening presents. After that his temper flared and Mom suggested Deena and I go for a walk. We'd felt so guilty, somehow, that we ended up sitting in the chapel watching the weak winter sunlight trying to make the stained-glass windows look like something holy.

"Sammie?" Mom was watching me. "What's on your mind?"

"Nothing." It wasn't fair to shatter the soft remembering mood that touched her and Deena's faces. I burrowed my toes beneath the shaggy bedside throw rug.

Mom patted the bed and I sat beside her. While Deena drank her orange juice, Mom's caring hands massaged my shoulders. "Last Christmas," she finally said, "was the saddest one in my life."

Deena sniffled.

Why had I looked at the picture? I tried to get up, but Mom's hands lingered.

"Your father cried after you girls left the room that day," she said quietly. "He felt absolutely terrible about spoiling your Christmas."

Guilt sliced right through me. So he'd cried too.

If he were alive I could get mad and yell at him, and then things would be all right. But he was dead. How could I be so awful to be mad at somebody who was *dead*?

"Oh Sammie, honey." Mom drew me into a hug. "It's all right."

I clung to her. And then Deena, still sniffling, joined us. "He tried," Mom said. "We all did the best we could."

I nodded, glanced at the picture once more. "I remember — " I gulped. "I remember when I was seven, and he made me that doll house for Christmas."

Mom ruffled my hair. "He worked on it for weeks, he was so determined to get it perfect for his little girl. And he was absolutely thrilled that you loved it so much."

"He never made *me* a doll house." Deena almost sounded put out, but I had a feeling it was a bluff.

"He made you a rocking horse. The year before, when you were three. You always played at being a cowboy. You rode it so hard you pulled off the mane and tail."

I shot a fake scowl at my sister. "You always were a wild little kid."

Deena gave us her angelic smile. "Who, me?"

After that everything was all right. Mom was touched by the pair of fur-lined moccasins I'd bought her with my baby-sitting money, and right away Deena buried her nose in the copy of *The Canadian Teen's Guide to Love and Beauty*, which I'd found at Coles. Meanwhile, tears came to my eyes when I opened a tiny package from Mom. A small gold-plated French horn pendant dangled from a delicate chain.

"Thanks, Mom," I choked.

Her eyes were warm on me. "It's not much, and I wish I could do a lot more."

It seemed to be a day for hugging. I threw my arms around Mom.

"I know it's not easy, Sammie," she said in my ear. "Especially when you can't even practise. But don't give up. Things will get better, just wait and see."

She almost sounded as if she had a plan up her sleeve, but before I had a chance to ask, the buzzer went and we were all still in our PJs. In the stunned silence Mom smoothed the turquoise robe she always wore for lounging around. "I'll get it," Deena announced, setting branches swaying as she rushed to the intercom.

"Ho! Ho! Ho! Merry Christmas!" Glenna's voice greeted us. A few minutes later they bustled in, Willie perched on Greg's arm as usual. "What, aren't you lazy people dressed yet?" Glenna cried. She handed Mom a foil-wrapped package. "We're on our way to Greg's parents'. I know this isn't much, but . . ."

"Oh, Glenna, you baked fruitcake? That's very thoughtful. I didn't have time this year." Mom was looking all mushy again.

"And I also wanted to ask you . . ."

The apartment went quiet except for ripping sounds as Willie discovered the cast-off wrapping paper.

" . . . if you wanted to come to the graveyard with us."

The air shimmered with something indefinable. My half-sister's face was solemn, a little nervous. Her dark eyes held an expression so much like Dad's in one of his serious moods. We looked at one another in a kind of silent communion so powerful I felt as if I could reach out and touch it.

"I'd like that," Mom said calmly after a moment. "Girls?"

It was hard for me to visit Dad's grave. Slowly I nodded. Deena had already pulled her jogging suit back over her pyjamas.

Sunlight rebounded off the snow. We parked the Toyota behind Greg's Chevy and got out. The air was cool and sweet; the massive Douglas fir and cedars surrounding the cemetery carried a kind of eternal wisdom that made my day-to-day life seem trivial. Here and there, alone or in small clusters, people came and went, remembering. I drew back at the thought of Dad's coffin, buried under-ground . . .

"You okay, kiddo?" Glenna grasped my elbow. I loved her for it, for noticing.

I looked at the footprints in the snow. Many graves hadn't been visited. Across the laneway where most of the markers were in Chinese, the thin layer of snow only partially covered a new mound of dirt and its floral arrangements.

Then I looked at the low headstone Glenna led me to: FRANKLIN. WILLIAM DELBERT. 1948-1991. BELOVED HUSBAND AND FATHER. A delicate layer of ice gleamed platinum on the granite surface, catching the sun and obscuring some of the letters. Mom knelt and brushed it off with her bare hand, then laid Deena's pine branch on the plot. We stood there. Willie's babbling blended with the chatter of the sparrows.

"He'd have liked knowing we all came here together," Mom said softly.

I looked at my mother standing there, the breeze playing with her wiry curls. She was still too thin, and sadness lurked in her eyes. Even so, she was calm and in control. How could she handle it so well? When my own emotions still bounced around like figures in a video game — just when you think you've finally got a handle on it, it comes up from behind and clobbers you all over again.

Glenna gave my elbow a squeeze. "I wish I could've known him better," she said.

I smiled weakly. Just living in the same house didn't guarantee you knew a person. It was things that weren't so obvious that mattered, not which brand of shaving cream he used, or what he'd say if you came in more than half an hour late.

Deena did a strange thing just then. She walked over to the gravestone and sat on it.

"Deena!" I choked. "Get off of there!"

Mom turned to me with a warning in her eyes.

"I feel closer this way," Deena explained. "Kinda like I'm sitting in his lap. He wouldn't mind."

I swallowed hard as Glenna laughed and agreed that Dad wouldn't mind.

A sick jealousy rocked me. I looked at the incredible beauty of sun on snow and felt cheated. "Scoot over," I told Deena, and sat beside her. But I didn't feel closer, just hard edges of cold stone pressing against my bum — which made me feel like such a baby that I got up and started walking away.

And then it happened. A feeling of peace settled around me, a quiet, loving feeling. Time stopped. The others were like statues in a garden. The quietness slid through me like warmth after having been out in the cold for too long. *Dad was all right. Somehow, somewhere, he still loved me. He was still there for me.* The awareness was so real it shimmered all about me, so beautiful I couldn't do anything but *be*. When it vanished as quickly as it had appeared, I was left with a feeling of calm that lingered deep inside.

"Would you like to go for a walk, Sammie?" Mom was asking.

The two of us wandered amongst the graves, not talking much. So many names carved in stone, so many people. It was humbling to think about. Someday Mom might be here. Maybe *I* would. The thought didn't scare me as much as it would have only a few hours ago. We were all part of something bigger, and dying was part of the pattern.

But when we came across a recent mound — a stone engraved with BRUCKNER. TAMARA LYN. 1977-1991. A SHINING LIGHT — I cried.

Six

*O*n Boxing Day Jennifer slept over. As we sprawled in sleeping bags, the Christmas tree lights on and my new k.d. lang tape playing softly, I haltingly told her about my experience at the cemetery. Somehow it helped me see things differently, thinking about Dad, and how life was now.

It was well past midnight. Jen yawned. An amber tree light reflected off her dark hair. "I'm so glad, Sammie. All that time — I mean, when he was so sick, well . . . it must really help you feel better." I suddenly realized that she'd hardly known Dad when he was still healthy. During that last year she'd only seen him once or twice when he was home on a pass.

I looked at the carpet to keep from thinking about the unhappy times. Tiny clots of lint cast shadows in the dim glow from the tree. The building was quiet, and the sirens and other city sounds seemed far away and not quite real. From the kitchen came the steady *plink, plink* of the faucet.

"I got that kind of peaceful feeling once," Jen murmured sleepily. "About my grandpa. He died when I was eight." She turned over, and in a minute her breathing changed to the slow, steady rhythm of sleep.

The music ended. I got up and put in Deena's favourite Colin James tape. As I snuggled back into my sleeping bag I wondered why Tamara Bruckner's grave had made me cry instead of Dad's, and wished I could've talked it through with Jen. But the whole Matt Bruckner thing was way outside her world.

"Wait, Ms. Barnett!" Deena yelled in her sleep. "I forgot!"

I smiled. My sister was haunted by her own ghosts, and some of them were very much alive.

A dream awakened me later.

Looking for Dad. Uncle Amos was going to build us a house, and he needed to measure Dad. As I wandered through our backyard, calling, I found Matt Bruckner waiting by the blackberry hedge. "I know where he is," Matt said. He led me through the brambles, through the fence, and then we were in a forested area. It was misty. Matt walked swiftly and I had to hurry to keep up. "Here," Matt said, pointing to a bed of ferns. But it was my French horn, not my father, that lay nestled in the lacy foliage. Then I was in a house. Old-fashioned fiddle music was coming from somewhere. I looked around and saw Dad playing in a rocking chair — only he was using Maestro's baton for a bow, and it wasn't really a violin at all, but some kind of car part.

I lay there in the dark listening to Jen's soft breathing. Upstairs somebody flushed a toilet. I wondered if Matt was beginning to adjust to his paralysis. And his sister's death.

My dream was still vivid when I awoke later to the sounds of Mom fixing coffee. I told her and Jen about it as I poured myself a bowl of Shreddies. As usual, Deena slept in.

Mom smiled, looking relaxed in her turquoise robe. "How is the Bruckner boy doing?"

I shook my head. I'd told Mom about the time we played at the hospital.

"That poor boy," she said. "Maybe he'll be transferred to the rehab hospital soon. He'll be much happier there."

Dad never made it to rehab. In spite of that long year in hospital. One reason was that he was dying, but it was also because of a long waiting list. I took a sip of coffee. "Do you think I should visit him again?"

Mom gave me a serious look. "I can't answer that for you, Sammie."

Jen stirred her cereal. "What about his other friends?"

From the looks of Matt's hospital room, you'd think he didn't have any friends. "How'm I supposed to know?" I said, and spread a huge glob of marmalade on my raisin toast.

Maybe Matt needed something funny to liven up the place. After all, with his family grieving over Tamara's death too, nobody would be feeling terribly upbeat. Dad's hospital room had always been cluttered with things we'd brought from home. Afterwards, all those things came back neatly packed in garbage bags. Two still sat in our storage unit, unopened.

"Sammie," Mom said, distracting me, "I admire you for this, but are you ready?" Her hand shook as she poured herself more coffee. "I don't want you hurt, love. Sometimes men can be so thoughtless when they're depressed."

I looked more closely at her. Tears were brimming in her hazel eyes. "Thank heaven your father got past that stage," she murmured. "We had some good talks before the end. He maybe didn't let you know, but he loved you girls very, very much."

I sniffled and hugged Mom tightly. As I glanced at Jen I noticed that she was folding her paper napkin again and again into tiny triangles.

* * *

Later we caught the downtown bus and got off at Haida Court, the city's classiest mall. We tried on sweaters and jeans in Eaton's, then wandered into the crowded mall for something to eat. Before we'd found a table, a pair of hands reached for my tray. "Ladies. Allow me."

My jaw dropped. "What do you think you're . . . !" Jen burst out.

Julie Blaustein stood there grinning, dressed like

a true preppy in a pleated wool skirt with leotard
and tights. "Ladies, I know the perfect place, away
from the trampling mob, away from the smoke and
litter. Would you care to join me?"

Jen was staring as if Julie were a bag lady in
mink. "Jen," I said quickly, "this is Julie Blaustein
from orchestra. Julie, this is my friend Jennifer
Cascardi."

"Hi," Julie said. "Seriously, I've found a cool
place, and I'm bored to death. I have to wait for my
mothah, who is having her *haih* done."

Jennifer shot me an uncertain look.

"Sure," I said.

But when I saw Julie's idea of a cool place, I had
second thoughts. Near the elevators and a small
B.C. Tel office, three stylized totem poles were
being installed, cordoned off by thick yellow rope
and moveable posts. Workmen's equipment lay
idle.

Julie slipped under the rope and leaned comfort-
ably against one of the totem poles. "See?" she
said. "Perfect place."

Jen made a show of looking at her watch. "I have
to be home by two," she lied.

A thunderbird scowled at us from the opposite
wall. "Won't we get kicked out?" I asked. But in a
way I was tempted. Julie had such a way of liven-
ing things up.

"We won't," Julie said. When Jen and I stared
blankly at her, she sighed. "My dear father, among
other things, owns this bloody mall. My dahling
mothah will take a hairy spazz — but it's her own

silly fault, since she insisted I wait for her 'on the premises.' She spends *hours* in that fruity salon."

I caught a surprised breath. Julie Blaustein's father owned the whole mall? At the same instant, something sparked inside me. Balancing my tray, I stepped over the rope and sat down. A frown puckered Jen's forehead but she followed.

"See?" Julie said triumphantly. "Isn't this better?"

I leaned against the carved fragrant wood of a totem pole, for an instant feeling like I was committing some terrible crime. But in a weird way Julie was right. Where we'd stood only minutes earlier, hordes of shoppers were shoving against one another, balancing food trays and over-stuffed shopping bags. Meanwhile an impossible line-up was forming outside the movie theatre.

"This place gives me the creeps," Jen mumbled, taking an enormous bite of her hot dog.

"Oh well," Julie said. "No harm done." She brushed the seat of her skirt just as a scowling security guard walked by. "These ladies are with me," she called out.

The guard ignored us totally.

Julie grinned. "Unreal, yes?"

Jen swallowed another gulp of hot dog. I glanced at Julie and grinned back. Suddenly I felt as if I could float away on the wonderful wacky feeling inside. "I want to look for a funny get-well card for Matt Bruckner," I said.

Julie sobered. Intent green eyes studied me. "Have you heard anything?"

"No." I took a long sip of Coke and explained about my two visits to the hospital.

Julie nodded, making me wonder whether she'd stepped in to see Matt the night we played there. "That kid," she said slowly, "had his hopes up for the 1994 Tchaikovsky Competition in Moscow. It'll be a miracle if he ever gets there now."

I winced. But Jen was looking impatient, so I followed her toward the escalator.

On our way we had to step aside for a woman in a motorized wheelchair. Her head lolled; her bent wrists looked impossibly stiff as she operated the controls with her fingertips. It obviously wasn't easy, with or without the shopping bags piled in her lap. An older woman walked by her side.

The three of us fell silent. The woman wasn't much older than Glenna. As I watched, four guys started sniggering and shoving each other around, making loud comments about which of them was going to do you-know-what to the woman in the chair.

I boiled, sick with anger. The poor woman's face went a mottled red. The companion bent to whisper something in her ear. Jennifer, looking totally embarrassed, started edging away.

"Wait." Julie's eyes snapped. Head high, sleek dark hair bouncing off her shoulders, she marched over to the leader of the group of boys and jabbed a finger in his chest. Her words were low and controlled and often unrepeatable. And they worked. The boys shuffled away and Julie Blaustein returned, head still high and face composed.

With its soft mechanical whine the wheelchair carried the woman into the crowd.

I was speechless.

"Pigs!" Julie spat out. "*Machismo ultimo*, the kind who'll grow up to guzzle their beer with the boys and borrowed ladies, while their wives stay home changing diapers and then get slapped around for complaining."

"I hate them!" Jen's cheeks were flaming. "That poor woman can't help the way she is!"

"Exactly," Julie muttered.

I wondered if Matt would get that kind of treatment once he got out of hospital — assuming he smartened up and did something about getting better. More memories surfaced. "When we went places with my dad, sometimes people would look at him like there was something wrong with his mind — just because he was in a wheelchair. And skinny, and sick . . ." The memories knotted my throat. "I hope Matt doesn't have to put up with that."

Julie inspected her fingernails. "He will. Until he learns to look people in the eye again and let them know he's as good as anybody else. And one hell of a lot better musician." A pensive look shadowed her face and her voice went flat. "What a waste."

I wondered what she was thinking, but Jen was glancing at her watch. "There's a gift shop over there. My mom . . ." I looked and saw silvery balloons perched on sticks.

"Eternal Celebrations," Julie said. "They'll have something."

Didn't Julie have anything better to do? It wasn't like Jen and I were fascinating company. Pushing back the thoughts, I went into the store.

"Oh, isn't this adorable?" Jen cried, stroking a fluffy white toy kitten with green glowing eyes. Then she saw the price tag. "Ugh. $27.95!"

I cringed. Julie's idea of affordable obviously would be different from Jen's and mine.

Julie fingered a display of zodiac necklaces. "Scorpio, that's me." She held one against her black leotard. "What do you think, Sammie?"

But I only glanced at it. Sitting on a glass shelf was a line of small stuffed animals, each holding a musical instrument. A bear with a trumpet in one paw. A kangaroo with a drum. A skunk — I sputtered with laughter. A skunk was playing a violin. It fit Matt's personality perfectly. I showed it to the others.

Jen giggled. "I'd never sit through *that* concert."

"Never mind the concert," Julie said. "What about the poor violin section? But let's see . . . These are fun."

Jen wandered off to check out some fluorescent pens. "Something like this would sure give Matt's room some personality," I said. "Not that I'd have the nerve to give him the skunk."

"Bad idea," Julie agreed. "He's really not that way, you know. When he cares about something, he *cares*. Intensely."

It made sense. I stroked an owl with a saxophone. $24.95. More than I could really afford. I needed to buy a bus pass for the new year. But still . . . And then, on the back of the shelf, I saw it. A monkey, eyes glinting with mischief, posed with a violin.

"Perfect," Julie announced.

"Hey, Jen," I called. "Can I borrow ten bucks until I baby-sit next Tuesday?"

She came over to look. "Oh, he's *darling*! But why not a French horn?" Then it dawned on her. "I thought you were just buying a card," she said suspiciously. "I mean, you don't even know the guy."

"Well — " I stroked the monkey's crinkly brown fur " — he needs *something*."

"Oh why not," Jen said after a pause. "I sure wouldn't want to be in his shoes."

Julie was already holding out a twenty dollar bill. "Count me in. It's a vital cause."

Something didn't feel quite right. After all, it had been *my* idea, and I would've paid Jen back. Suddenly it was hard to meet Julie's eyes.

"Oh God," Julie groaned as the cashier put the monkey into a plastic bag. "The lady herself approacheth."

"*Juliet*," a voice said crisply as we stepped away from the till. "I've been looking all over for you."

Jen stepped on my heel when I didn't move ahead. A platinum blonde with sparkling fingers and earlobes, a formidable figure draped in mink, was looking down her nose at us.

"It's nice you've found some of your little friends," said the woman. "But we really *must* move along. Your lesson begins in half an hour, and I've telephoned James to bring the car."

I could see where Julie's exaggerated accent came from. The only place I'd heard anything like it was in the old black-and-white movies on TV.

Julie's face was an impassive mask. "Yes, Mother." She turned to me as she straightened her skirt. "Call me sometime," she hissed. "Things get pretty *much* around our place, if you know what I mean. Number's unlisted, so don't lose this." She slipped something into the bag.

"Do come along now, Juliet." Her mother's voice had a decided edge. I had to remind myself that those hard gems glittering in her face were really eyes.

I shivered, suddenly acutely aware of my faint resemblance to my great-great-grandmother, daughter of a runaway slave, and of Jennifer's classic Italian looks. Aware, too, of our worn jeans and sweatshirts, and our runners, which had long ago lost their pristine whiteness.

"Yes, Mother." Julie rolled her eyes and followed her mother.

Jen and I staggered out of the gift shop. I felt as if I'd been hit by a blast of polar wind.

Seven

"*I* feel like I've been hexed by the Wicked Witch of the West!" Jen said, tracing her toes in circles on the imitation marble floor.

"No — wrong book. Remember Narnia? She's the White Witch. You know, the one who makes it always winter but never Christmas." How could anybody tolerate a mother like that? No wonder Julie Blaustein acted weird.

I pulled the monkey out of the bag. Its comic face helped dispel some of the frigid feeling. With it came a lavender card that said simply, "Julie," and gave a telephone number, complete with area code. Weird, just like a business card. I ticked the edge of the card against a trash bin, then drew back.

Was that what Matt would do with the monkey? Trash it? You didn't give stuffed animals to six-teen-year-old guys. Especially ones who lay there, paralyzed, behind closed doors. Why had I let a stupid dream influence me? I'd already done more than half the kids in orchestra. "Let's go and get this over with," I mumbled.

Jennifer looked up in alarm. "You're not expecting *me* to come, are you?"

My stomach sank. "Please, Jen? You don't have to go to his room, just wait in the lobby. After that woman I . . ." At the moment I just couldn't face the hospital alone.

Jen kicked the bench leg. "Remember, I'm babysitting the Campbell brats tonight. I don't want to waste my whole day."

We took the bus down to the waterfront. The snow had melted, leaving everything soggy. Swollen clouds hung low over the strait; the water was grey-green and restless. In the distance Frigate and Cormorant Islands were low rounded shapes huddled beneath the raw sky.

Jennifer pulled a red toque out of her pocket and put it on. "I don't know about that Julie," she said as we walked along the breakwater.

Leaning out over the railing, I was torn between defending Julie and wanting to gossip. The wind whipped my hair back from my face, played with the loose cords on my jacket.

Jen picked at her curls, breaking off split ends. "You and me, we've been best friends forever. I feel like she wants a piece of that — and she seems the kind who'll go and take whatever she wants."

I thrust my cold hands into my pockets. "I bet she's lonely," I hedged. "Look at how her mom stared at us. Would *you* want to hang around, with that kind of treatment?"

"No way!" Jen propped her elbows on the rail. "Probably I'm just being stupid," she said, "but it seems like all you ever talk about now is that Matt guy. Plus your dad, of course."

A confused sensation left me hot and uncomfortable. I watched a tug pulling a CN barge. It was going so slowly it hardly seemed to move. The drone of the engine reminded me of an oversized bumblebee.

Finally I turned back to Jen. "You don't have to come to the hospital. I mean, it's my thing, not yours."

Her dark eyes looked embarrassed. She kicked at a metal post. "I didn't mean it like that. I'm sorry. I never should've said anything. It's dumb anyway."

I shoved against her shoulder. "Jennifer Cascardi, don't *be* like that! You're my *friend*. Best friends are supposed to tell each other everything. Even the hard stuff." Putting words to it helped me understand. Was Jen jealous? Of Julie? All the business about Matt?

Emotion washed through me. "You're the best friend I've ever had," I said in a low voice. "I never could've made it through all that time with Dad, without you."

She shrugged. "You would've — you're strong." But she straightened up, a slim dark-haired figure silhouetted against the dull sky and water. She smiled. "Come on, let's go."

The Dominion Avenue bus swept us away from the waterfront and up the hill. Crumpled newspapers scuttled across sidewalks as we passed; pedestrians scurried along, collars raised against the biting wind. When the bus pulled over at the hospital I was tempted not to get off. Jen glanced at me, her dark eyes questioning. I reached inside the plastic bag and took courage from the furry touch of the monkey.

As I walked down the bright corridor, alone, the monkey seemed more and more preposterous. What was I supposed to do, set it on the bedside table? Hand it to him? To Matt Bruckner, who couldn't care less if I walked in? I wished Julie were with me. With her funny up-front way of saying things, it would be a cinch to walk into Matt's room.

At first glance I thought he wasn't there. The bed was empty. The wheelchair was empty. And there was little in the room to show that it was occupied — though a triangular hoist now dangled from a bar that ran the length of the bed. They'd put one over Dad's bed too, so he could pull himself into a sitting position.

I gulped in a deep breath, realizing I'd be able to get away without having to face him.

"Help!"

The cry came from the other side of the bed.

I found Matt sprawled on the floor at the foot of his wheelchair. "What on earth happened?" I said. "Are you all right?"

His skinny face was streaked with sweat, and he looked mad enough to bite a snake. The feeding tube still dangled from his nose, but it wasn't hooked up to anything. The loose end was taped shut and pinned to his hospital pyjamas.

Matt tried to raise himself on his elbows. "I was trying to get back into bed," he said in a tight, furious voice.

"Are you all right?" I said again. Quickly I thought back to the times I'd helped Dad transfer in and out of his chair. But this was different. Matt was on the floor, in a heavy cast. All his weight was on the floor and I'd have to —

"Those nurses!" he fumed, swearing. "They make me sit so long my back hurts. I yelled but nobody came. Couldn't reach the bloody call button, so I decided to try it myself."

"How long ago did you fall?" I knelt on the floor beside him.

Matt's brown eyes were dark with anger. "They call this place a hospital. Doctors and nurses and lab techs jabbing at you every second, but the minute you need one, forget it!"

I extended my hands. "Here — can you roll toward me? I'll see if — "

"It takes two to lift me," he said scornfully.

I hesitated, wondering if I should tell him about Dad. "Well, one's better than none, right?"

"It takes two. You'd probably drop me and turn me into a quadriplegic."

Serve you right, I thought. I took a steadying breath and set the bag and monkey on the bedside table. "I used to help lift my dad," I mumbled.

"So?" Matt grimaced as he tried to shift his position. His long legs were flopped out like cast-off mannequin parts and didn't move. "Was he a drunk or something?"

I had the strongest urge to kick Matt Bruckner as he lay there on the floor. Instead, I rocked to my feet, so mad I could hardly see straight. "Good luck," I said between clenched teeth, and punched the call button on my way out.

But nobody was at the nursing station. The hallway was empty, not even any visitors to tell. I only got halfway to the elevator before turning back to Matt's room.

"My father was paraplegic," I told him flatly. "Before he died of cancer."

"Sorry," he muttered. "I shouldn't've said that." He looked terribly uncomfortable. His robe and hospital pyjamas couldn't hide the catheter tube leading to the bag, which lay flat on the bed. He strained, lifting one leg with both hands so that it lay beside the other.

Tears sprang into my eyes. So many times I'd watched Dad move one or both legs that way, as if they were heavy meaningless weights. So many times I'd seen that same grimace. Again I held out both hands. "I'll help you up."

His eyes were tortured. "I told you, it takes two."

I drew in another long breath. "There's nobody at the nursing station. And the hall's empty. So it's just me — unless you want me to get my friend Jennifer in the lobby."

Matt swore.

"Come on, grab my wrists and let's see what we can do."

His fingers were like claws against my skin. I braced myself and pulled. He was all dead weight. Trembling with the strain, I hovered there, nearly falling on top of him. And then he let go. I sat down hard on the floor.

"Sorry," he mumbled again. "That won't work. Let me hold onto your shoulders. That's how the nurses do it."

He caught my shoulders and hung on, panting, as I cautiously shifted my position. Like I'd done so many times with my father, I pressed my knees against his limp ones to keep them from buckling. If I could just get him into the wheelchair . . . His heavy cast clanked against the bed rail. But his legs were slipping . . .

"What's going on in here?"

I looked up at the curt voice. Matt's hands slid off my shoulders, and there was a heavy thud that shook the floor. Some very unmuffled swearing. I winced and wished I could be anyplace else — down at the breakwater, even at the mall facing Julie's horrible mother.

The nurse pushed me aside to check on Matt. Then she turned on me with icy blue eyes. "You've no business moving him! *Always* call a nurse. He could've been hurt badly."

"I've been calling for the last hour!" Matt yelled. His nose tube jiggled with every word. "Nobody came. Where were you all, gossiping over coffee?"

"There was an emergency on the other wing," the nurse said coldly. "We're understaffed — you can't expect miracles, you know." She turned on me again. "You still should have asked for help. You've no business taking matters into your own hands."

"But — " Tears rushed to my eyes.

Matt interrupted me. "I was on the floor when she came in. My back got sore, sitting in that idiot chair, so I tried transferring myself. My parents'll have a lawyer in here this afternoon. Abandoning sick people. What a crock."

The nurse sighed and turned to me. "If you'd step out for a minute — "

"It takes two." Matt's retort lashed out at the nurse. "And I want to get back in bed *now*, not in another three weeks when the rest of you guys decide to come back from holidays."

"Want some help?" I offered. "I know what to do."

The nurse sighed again. "All right."

Once back in bed, Matt had the same skinny old-man look. He was nothing like the Matt from my dream, who'd led me through the forest to find my horn. This one stared into space as if I didn't even exist.

Nervousness skittered through me on tiny cockroach feet. The yellow plastic bag containing the monkey mocked me. Even though I could still pretend it was mine, I could hardly back down now. "Feeling better?" I asked.

Matt only swore.

I bit down hard. It was getting to be too much. "I hope you get into rehab soon," I said in a final attempt.

Matt gave a bitter laugh. "Just what I always wanted — life as a gimp."

"My dad learned to get around in a chair," I mumbled. "And he never made it to rehab. But he'd get day passes and go places . . ." It felt like such a feeble attempt.

"Oh sure. Must've done him one hell of a lot of good. He died, right?" Matt's eyes were as hard as Mrs. Blaustein's. With his cynical look and his shaggy reddish hair tousled against the pillow, he was a total stranger. This person could never, ever have sat in Youth Orchestra, and certainly had never made a violin sing.

"I have to go," I said, and ducked out as if a swarm of hornets was after me.

"Thanks for dropping by, Sam."

He didn't say it until I was in the hallway. Something warm touched my knotted, screaming insides. "See you," I said, and blew my nose so a passing dietitian might think my sniffles were just a cold. But my eyes were way too watery. Jen would know the difference. For sure.

Eight

*J*ulie cornered me in the rehearsal hall just before our first practice after Christmas holidays. "What did he think of the monkey?" she asked. Her green eyes sparked with an emotion I couldn't identify.

I'd been wondering the exact same thing for two weeks. "I don't know," I said. "He'd fallen on the floor, so I just set it on the table."

Julie drew in a sharp breath. "He wasn't hurt, was he?"

"No." As I recalled the frustrated anger in Matt's face, I thought about all the other ways of hurting.

Maestro was at the podium, rapping his baton. We hurried to our seats.

It was a grim rehearsal. After warmup Maestro told us to get out the Beethoven symphony. A feeling of dread washed over me. The French horn parts were wicked. Halfway through, we had a crucial passage. And we botched it. We cowered, even Troy, who played first horn and was terrific.

Maestro's baton slashed the air like a white bayonet. "French horns!" he barked. "What exactly do you mean by that?"

All around us kids shifted in their seats. Amy set her flute across her lap and began digging in her purse. Beside me, Duane blew water out of his trumpet. My horn was full of moisture too; I needed to pull some valve slides to empty them, but there was no way I'd try it with Maestro glaring at us.

"Play it again. The four of you."

My heart thudded nervously. My upper lip was puffy and numb from playing. With a touch of bitterness, I thought about how I hated that apartment, where I wasn't allowed to practise. It wasn't *my* fault my lip muscles were weak. All the other kids got plenty of practice and most took private lessons, as well.

Maestro gave the upbeat. My lip struggled to make the fine adjustments for changing pitch as we played the passage. At my left, Arthur's tone cracked on a simple D an octave above middle C. Jason's horn gurgled. My own part was in an easy low register, but my lip was losing its flexibility so fast my notes came out tight and strained.

"What?" Maestro roared. "You have the nerve to call that *music*? Again. *Play* it."

We did. Again, and again, so many times I began feeling like a whipped dog. Even that didn't satisfy Maestro. "What's the matter with you people?" he raged. "The passage is not impossible. You're wasting our time. The others know their parts. Is there any reason the French horns should be exempt?" He scowled at the clock. "Troy. Play it."

Sweat erupted all over me. Maestro *never* singled people out to play alone, not unless he was really worked up. When he did, he was ruthless.

Even Troy sounded scared. Maestro let him get by with playing it twice, plus some barbed comments. Jason rushed his part, missing notes and making mistakes in his tonguing. I used the time to empty my horn. I was holding it upside down, dribbling water out, when Maestro started in on Arthur. Furtively I massaged my lip. There was almost no sensation left.

"Samantha!" Maestro barked, after lambasting Arthur about his breathing technique. I looked into those fierce eyes and nearly cried. Trash, that's what he thought we were. He gave the downbeat.

I faltered. My tired lip allowed only a muffled blatty tone to escape. I pressed the mouthpiece tighter, so hard it felt as if I were jamming my teeth backwards. A few more wimpy notes came out, and then nothing, just air. I sat there, sweltering. Maestro hurled his baton across the room. *"Really!"* His acid tone dissected me into tiny fragments of prickling shame. "I have never heard such exquisite playing in my entire life."

Hot tears spilled down my face, but I didn't dare put my hands up to hide them, or even to rummage in my purse for a tissue.

Maestro seemed not to notice. The scathing

words continued. "Is that all you can offer us? What good is that? I presume you consider yourself sufficiently talented, having earned a position in this orchestra, that you no longer need stoop to practise. *Really*!"

With a violent sweep he flung the musical score onto the floor. The fluttering papers startled the pulsating silence in the room. "You have two weeks, Samantha. I will listen to you privately after each rehearsal. If there is no improvement, a replacement will be found."

I dropped my face into my hands and clenched my teeth to choke back the sobs. All around came muted sounds of scraping chairs, instrument cases clicking shut. Nobody was talking much.

"Oh Sammie!" Hilary's soft voice was so sympathetic I cried harder, especially when her hand came to rest gentle and warm on my shoulder. "That man is awful!" she whispered. "He has no feelings at all."

I needed something to lean on, but it might have looked strange if I'd cried all over Hilary, so I rested my head on my cold black music stand. So what if I got the music wet? Things couldn't get any worse. In two weeks I wouldn't need it anyway.

"He yelled at me like that once in grade nine," Renée said. I heard her pull up a chair and sit down. "But afterwards, he was nicer — if that helps any." She sounded terribly nervous.

I didn't know what to say. There just weren't any words for how I felt, and I couldn't turn it off and laugh, or make a mad dash out to the street. In one of the adjoining rooms I could hear Julie's indignant voice defending me. I felt so awful I didn't even want to listen.

Hilary patted my shoulder. "Let's go to the washroom. And don't worry. You'll do fine, I know you will."

I pulled myself together enough to pack my horn away, and made a point of avoiding everybody as we walked by.

Renée followed. "How are you going to find a place to practise, Sammie? Will they let you at school?"

I cupped my hands in the cool water and swished it over my burning eyes again and again. "Maybe," I mumbled. "I'll have to ask if I can use the music room at lunch." Actually, that might be the answer — but if Jennifer felt left out now, this would only make things worse. And if I could just find a way to work it through without telling Mom . . . She'd been awfully worn out since the beginning of the new year. Some days at breakfast she looked as if she hadn't slept all night. If she found out about this, she'd probably blame herself, for moving us to the crummy apartment in the first place. Then another thought struck me, and I laughed wildly.

"If my mother hears about this," I gasped, "my aunt will find out, and then I'll be stuck practising at *her* house."

"Good!" Hilary said eagerly.

I clutched the porcelain sink and groaned. "You

wouldn't say that if you knew my aunt and my cousin." I could just see Aunt Vivian, hovering in the next room the way she used to when Blake took violin. Any time there was silence — or wrong notes, or anything that didn't sound like a music lesson — her nagging would fill the house. And the idea of practising where Blake would be in and out was positively repulsive.

There was a sudden banging on the washroom door. "Can I come in?" Julie called.

Hilary looked at me with a question in her dark eyes. I nodded.

Julie burst in. "I told that man!" she said. "I told him about your problem with the apartment. And I told him if he kicks you out, I'll organize a strike."

I stared. So did Hilary and Renée. Julie's father was chairman of the symphony board. Even so, she was taking things a bit far.

"Uh-oh," Renée said, enunciating each syllable.

"Don't do that," I begged.

Julie shrugged. "I already said I would. That man is top of the line musically, but sometimes his methods stink."

"It won't come to that," Hilary said in a hurry. "Sammie thinks she'll be able to practise at school, or at her aunt's." She turned to me. "My father must be here by now. Want a ride home?"

Hilary's father was a small, pleasant-looking man whose hair was thinning on top. In his Chinese-accented voice he cheerfully agreed to drive me home, pretending not to notice my red eyes. I sank back against the seat. It felt good to be going someplace with a father driving — even if it was somebody else's father. Dad had been sick for so long before his final ten months in hospital that it seemed forever since we'd gone anywhere with him in the driver's seat. And then another thought slipped idly into my mind, surprising me. Wouldn't Mom start dating eventually? Not that she'd find anybody like Dad, but . . .

In the front seat Hilary and her father were speaking Chinese. As we stopped at a red light, Mr. Wong turned to me with a sympathetic look. "I think sometimes your director isn't very kind. Hilary practises many, many hours. She tries very hard to play perfectly, but he never says, 'That's good.'"

"But he's never been terrible like with Sammie," Hilary cut in. "He was *awful*. He made everybody feel bad."

Once again tears welled into my eyes.

"That's bad if there is no place for you to play," Hilary's father said thoughtfully. He straightened up just as the light changed. "I have an idea. You ask your mother. You can play at our house every time after the orchestra practice. My wife will fix you something to eat, and then we'll give you a ride home."

I was overwhelmed. For the plan to work I'd still have to check with Mom. She might pull the Aunt Vivian number on me, but it was worth a try.

Mom was furious when she heard the news. "Since when is it all right for someone to humiliate my daughter like that? It's not *your* fault our nice middle-class environment went down the tubes.

I'm going to call that man and tell him a thing or two!" The warm aroma of macaroni and cheese permeated the apartment. Through the ceiling came a loud scraping sound as the people upstairs pulled out their chairs to sit down to eat. Next door I could hear the Wallaces' TV turned up loud for the six o'clock news.

Mom's anger was unsettling. There was so much strain in her face. Even her skin was a tired colour. Being mad made it stretch so tightly across her cheekbones that I almost thought her face would split.

"Mom," I mumbled, "he'll only get madder. I sounded awful. It's just the way he *did* it." I pressed my lips together. I had to stay as calm as possible so Mom wouldn't worry.

Deena was leaning against the kitchen counter. "Why don't you quit if he's such an old geek? Get everybody else to quit, too. Then they'll have to hire somebody new."

"I can't quit *orchestra*." There was no way I could explain to Deena about orchestra. How it was the one thing that kept my life from getting bogged down in the dull routine of school. Through orchestra I could reach for something better, something special. It had to do with the way I felt inside, with music all around me, the way the air trembled with sound, even the floor. There was something awesome about how an orchestra could turn black notes on paper into living music, which transcended what any of us could ever be alone.

"It's not that simple, Deena," Mom said crossly.

"Your father and I wanted so much for you girls. Your sister's worked very hard. There is no way she should have to suffer that kind of abuse just because your father's death took away what most people take for granted." She banged a spatula onto the countertop so hard the thin metal neck snapped. The head skated across the smooth Formica, then clattered onto the floor. I stared at the decapitated handle.

"Holy, Mom!" Deena said after a stunned silence. "Are you ever strong!"

Suddenly Mom's chin was trembling. She turned away from us and slammed both fists hard against the refrigerator. "Everybody says I'm strong." The words came out measured, with ominous control, but in a little-girl voice. They came out accentuated by bangs on the fridge. "'You're so strong, Carolyn,' they all say. 'I don't see how you do it.' I can't be strong *all* the time, damn it! I *can't*! It hurts me so to see you girls suffer." Mom slumped against the refrigerator, weeping.

"Mom!" Deena gasped.

It was all my fault. Sobbing, I went to my mother and held her tightly.

Nine

*A*unt Vivian telephoned me the next day before Mom got home from work. She got straight to the point. "Sammie dear, you must realize your poor mother is a nervous wreck. With all she's been through, you really shouldn't bother her with your problems at school."

I opened my mouth to protest, but she continued like an oncoming tank. "She's reached the end of her rope, dear. Your mother is tremendously strong, but she hasn't given herself a chance to rest after the long ordeal of your poor father's illness. I keep telling her she ought to consider taking some time off, move in with us for a while, but no, she won't hear of it, insists on standing on her own two feet."

"I know she's really worn out," I said lamely, at the same time trying to digest the appalling idea — move in with *Aunt Vivian*? Thank goodness Mom kept saying no! I flicked the long telephone cord in waves, then twirled it like a jump rope. "I tried not to . . ."

"Come to me with your problems, Sammie."

"Mom!" Blake's voice bellowed, a distant presence at the other end of the line. "I can't find any underwear. And didn't you wash my shirt, you know, the — "

"Excuse me, dear," my aunt said crossly. "I'll be right back, so don't hang up."

I gritted my teeth and crossed my eyes at Deena, who was leaning against the kitchen counter and listening unabashedly. It would serve Aunt Vivian right if I did hang up, the old bat. The nosy, gossipy . . .

Deena grinned. "I'm glad it's you she's talking to, not me. I can hear her all the way over here."

"I bet." I dangled the receiver by the cord, letting it bounce gently against the floor, and rubbed my ear with my free hand. Aunt Vivian's tinny telephone voice had a way of penetrating deep into my head, giving me an earache.

"Here, catch!" Deena tossed me a banana.

I took a big bite. Without warning, Aunt Vivian crackled out of the phone down by the floor. "Sorry," I mumbled, mouth full. "I didn't hear what you said."

There was an exasperated sigh. "I was saying, I want you girls to come to me with your problems. Tell Deena that too. She's the one your mother worries about — won't settle down, get serious about anything."

Deena scowled and made a threatening gesture

with her banana. "Tell that to your darling Blakie, Auntie V," she mimicked in a voice too low to reach the phone. Ever since Christmas dinner, when Blake had been a total jerk, Deena had gone around making up gross rhymes about our cousin.

I swallowed the clump of banana faster than I would have liked. "You don't need to worry about the practising," I said. "I can use the music room at lunch. And I'll be going to Hilary's after each orchestra rehearsal."

My aunt made a sound that closely resembled a *humpf.* "I really don't think you should be imposing on other families, dear. You come here to practise. We'll work something out."

I kicked the legs of the stool. "I've already *got* it worked out. Mom thinks it's fine. She said — "

"She's also on the edge of a nervous breakdown, if you ask me. We have to protect her from any unnecessary stress."

"Yes, Aunt Vivian."

"I'm glad you understand. I'll clear out some space in Amos's workshop. We'll be expecting you tomorrow after school." She hung up with a decisive click.

The next day I left my French horn at school and made a point of walking to The Junction with Jen once classes got out. After all, since we hadn't eaten lunch together, it was important to catch up on everything — right?

"There's Adam!" Jennifer cried, pointing to a passing car.

Shock waves jangled through me. At the same instant came the deep horn blast of the four o'clock ferry as it began gliding away from the terminal.

Jen giggled. "Can't say the guy has no effect on you."

My cheeks went hot, but I was too busy looking to answer her. The car was going slowly down Dominion Avenue, and it was packed so full of guys they were hanging out the windows. There was Adam in the back seat with his head and elbow sticking out. He was wearing his red hockey jacket.

I waved. So did Jen.

Whistles and yells erupted from the car, but most of the guys were looking the other way. Adam lifted his hand in a brief salute, then turned. On the other side of the street Charmaine was walking with April McLeod. The two of them might as well have been on TV, they were looking so great — alive and on top of it all. As I watched, Adam put his fingers to his lips and whistled.

"Huh," Jennifer muttered. "See if we ever speak to *you* again, Charmaine Phelps!"

I tried not to let it bother me. Once we got to The Junction I'd order a large hot chocolate with double whipped cream. And then I'd talk to Jen about . . . about what? The whole thing with Mom was a little scary, and private. You didn't go around telling your friends you were afraid your mother was about to crack up. So instead, I listened. Jen went on and on about Tomás Díaz, the new student in her computer class. And she was worried about our writing assignment for English.

I was late getting home. So was Mom.

"Where've you *been*?" Deena really looked put out. "Aunt Vivian phoned a million times, wondering when you were coming."

I groaned and flung my backpack onto the couch. "How'd Uncle Amos ever get stuck with such a bossy old witch? No wonder he's on his boat half the time."

Deena snickered. "I bet she got pregnant." Then she ran a hand through her hair, making it stick out wildly. "She wants you to call the minute you get home. 'Now you tell your sister I've been expecting her,'" she went on, mimicking. "'I went to a lot of trouble to fix up a place for her to practise, and she ought to be grateful.'"

I sputtered, caught between laughter and indignation.

Deena's eyes widened as I walked over to the phone. "You're actually gonna do it?"

I shook my head and set the receiver on top of the fridge. The dial tone hummed into the kitchen, followed by the recording telling me to please hang up and try my call again. When I didn't, an irritating series of beeps chattered at us.

Deena looked at me. We giggled. "Serves her right," she said. "Why didn't *I* think of that?"

"C'mon," I said. "Let's see what's in the fridge. We can fix supper and save Mom some hassle."

When Mom finally came in it was nearly seven o'clock. Her face was pale with fatigue, but her eyes were animated. Hyper. "Sorry I'm so late," she said. "Some things came up. I tried calling, but couldn't get through — and you've cooked dinner? Oh girls, I knew I could count on you!" She hugged each of us and set her purse down.

I watched Mom and her quick erratic movements. Any time she was this hyper it meant she had news of some kind.

"I hope you girls will forgive me." Her voice sounded strange. Excited, nervous. "I've — " She broke off. "What's the phone doing on the refrigerator?"

Deena and I glanced at one another.

"It's my fault," I said quickly.

"Aunt Vivian," Deena explained. "She kept calling the whole stupid afternoon, bugging me. And Sammie was late, and Aunt V just kept calling. I hate her."

Mom's mouth quirked. "No wonder I couldn't get through," she said drily. She started toward the phone, then sat down instead. "Girls, I have something to tell you. I'm not sure you're going to like this, but . . ." She hesitated as if she really didn't want to pass on the news. "Maybe we should eat first, since you girls went to all the trouble of cooking."

"Mom!" Deena cried. "Don't *be* like that!"

"Sorry." Mom smiled in a strange, embarrassed way.

I caught my breath. It must be a man. She was going to tell us about someone we'd be seeing a lot of in the future. A sudden resentment burst inside me. It was almost a year now since Dad's death, and it was probably time . . .

"I've talked to the Townsends," Mom said. "I'm putting our house up for sale." She paused, looked at us. "And I've sold the car," she added sheepishly.

"What?" My mouth sagged open. A strange blankness inside prevented thoughts from forming.

"What'd you go and do that for?" Deena wailed. "I mean, selling the house isn't so bad, but we need the car!"

"Not as badly as we need a house." There was a funny little smile on Mom's face. "We all hate this rabbit cage. Don't you think it's time we had a place we can call home?"

"Yeah, but you said you were selling — "

"I thought we didn't have enough — "

Pieces of questions cluttered the air. Little by little Mom pieced the story together. By selling the car and borrowing from Uncle Amos, she'd scraped together enough to make a down payment on a handyman's special. "It's not very big," she said. "And it needs a lot of work." The way housing prices had shot up, our old house was worth a lot of money. Once it sold and that mortgage was paid off, we'd have enough cash left to just about pay off the new house. And she'd gotten a raise at work. She'd also found a job waitressing evenings and weekends. "Just until the house sells," she promised. "You girls are too important to leave completely on your own." Mom chattered on and on about things like paint and wallpaper and carpets. "The floors slant, and it has an old oil furnace in the living room." She paused and looked at us. "The house is on Helm Street, in the Harbour District."

The Harbour District. It was a rougher part of town. On the other hand, we'd be close to Glenna.

Mom was looking at us seriously, trying to connect. "The realtor will be here in an hour," she said. "Her name is Mrs. Raymond, and she'll take us over to look at the place. If you girls don't like it I want you to let me know *immediately*, while I still have a chance to get the car back. The whole deal is conditional for the next twenty-four hours."

"What's Aunt Vivian gonna think?" Deena whispered.

Mom's head lifted proudly. "She can think whatever she likes. Amos understands. It's *our* life, not theirs."

The real estate agent was a middle-aged woman with an expensive car and a fake smile. Some instinct told me not to trust her. My throat caught as Deena and I slid into the back seat of the big Oldsmobile. I'd gotten fond of our Toyota, and I'd been hoping to learn to drive soon. As we swooped under the streetlights, the powerful engine barely audible, I felt as nervous as during some of Dad's medical crises. Sure, we hated the apartment, but the Harbour District? I wouldn't have to change schools, but still . . . Lurking behind everything was a sadness at letting go of the house on Glencairn Road. Where we'd all been together, with Dad, and happy. I'd always hoped somehow we could move back there. Now it was goodbye for sure.

Mom was right. The house *was* small. In the dark I couldn't really tell what colour it was, only that the paint was peeling. The agent muttered and turned on a flashlight so she could see to open the lock box. It was hard to see much of the neighbourhood, except that there were big trees and old houses, and parked cars that didn't look in the greatest shape.

"Here we are," the agent said in a cheery tone, reaching in to turn on some lights.

Our feet made hollow clomping sounds as we walked around. The air had a stale, musty smell. The floor squeaked, and as Mom had said, it slanted. Discoloured old-fashioned wallpaper clung to the walls, peeling in a few spots. The paint on the windowsills was chipped, and in the kitchen one wall was caked with grease where the stove had been. There were two bedrooms, bigger than what we had in the apartment, but the closets weren't any better. The whole house felt cold and damp.

Deena and I looked at one another.

"This place would be really sweet fixed up," the lady gushed. "With the furnace going it'll be nice and cozy; in a few years you might want to replace it with a modern one. Some people are putting in those nice wood stoves . . . The walls are sound." She knocked on one, as if to prove her point. "And look — " She pointed out carved designs in the door frames. "You won't see this in just any house. This house is a hundred years old. Back then they took care to put in extra finishing touches. The last owners let it slide, but with some work — stripping the paint, new wallpaper, replacing the carpet — you could end up with some valuable property.

More and more people are moving into this part of town and upgrading these old homes. In a few years this will be a really nice area, the old homes and big trees — the atmosphere, you know."

The woman went on and on as if she'd been wound up like a toy. I wished she had batteries that I could take out. Or that I could stuff her in the trunk of her Oldsmobile so we could look at the place in peace.

Mom kept glancing at Deena and me with a pinched, eager expression. "There are windows on all four sides," she murmured. "Natural light any time of day. Nobody stomping over our heads at ungodly hours. No sounds of other people's plumbing. Or smells of their cooking."

"Yeah," Deena muttered. "And what kind of people live next door? Winos? Rapists? And how are we supposed to get anyplace with no car?"

Something happened to Mom's face. It was as if a light went out. "There's a bus stop two blocks away," she said. "And you have a bicycle." She turned to the agent. "Please, could we have a few minutes to discuss this privately?"

"Oh, of course." With swishing skirt and mincing high-heeled steps, the woman stepped outside.

I felt like pounding Deena — not that I was crazy about the house, myself. And then I remembered something. "Didn't Dad grow up in this neighbourhood?" I blurted out.

"Yes, he did." Mom was trying very hard to keep the emotion out of her face, out of her voice. She really wanted us to make up our own minds.

Deena had an ominous sulky look.

"I know!" I said. "Mom and I can move here, and Deena, you can go live with Aunt Vivian."

Deena sputtered. "Go sit on a sea urchin. Share your bath with a jellyfish."

"Okay, okay. I get the idea." I turned to Mom. "Glenna hasn't mentioned any problems with things getting ripped off. Or derelicts on the streets."

"Just the sailors on leave," Deena countered.

I could've kicked her. "That would be right down your alley," I said. "They couldn't be any worse than that scrungy Leroy Pettigrew you're always watching for in the elevator."

Deena nearly went purple. And suddenly Mom looked so tired I halfway expected her to keel over. "This conversation is getting us nowhere," she said wearily. "The obvious thing to do is to go and ask for the car back."

"No!" I cried. "*Anything* would be better than the apartment."

Deena kicked at the worn, stained carpet. "At least this is farther from Aunt Vivian's," she muttered.

A foghorn bellowed suddenly, a raw, open sound.

"How close is the water?" I asked.

Mom rubbed her temples. "I'm not sure. The shipyards are over in that direction . . ." She gestured beyond the kitchen. "And my guess is it's ten or twelve blocks to that small park near the breakwater." She sighed. "I really wish you girls could've seen it in the daylight. You might have had a different impression. I really thought — "

"*I* think we should take it." I scowled at Deena.

"Fine," she said. "Then don't complain if we have rats for roommates."

Mom looked on the verge of tears. "I'm sorry, girls. I never should've sprung it on you like this. We should have discussed it first. There just wasn't time. And I'm afraid we can't keep Mrs. Raymond waiting outside indefinitely."

"She might get mugged," Deena said under her breath. But then she forced a smile. "Why not," she said. "Like you always say, paying rent is just throwing money away. We could make this place look cool. It might even be fun."

Impulsively I flung my arms around my sister. Unlike me, Deena would have to change schools. Maybe she hadn't realized that yet. "Aunt Vivian's going to have a cow," I said. And I laughed.

Mom wiped tears from the corners of her eyes. "Sammie, if you would, please make an effort to practise over there once in a while. She means well, really. And let's not say anything about this just yet. We'll let Amos tell her — all right?"

"No problem," said Deena. "If I got my way, I'd never say a *word* to Aunt V."

I looked around the old rundown house. Actually, Deena and the agent were both right. We really could make it look nice. It would be great to have a place to call home. "When do we move?" I asked.

Mom smiled. "In six weeks, if all goes well."

Ten

*E*verything went wild after that. Mom started waitressing right away, and most nights she didn't get home till eleven. I went through the motions of school, practising at lunch, then lugging my horn over to Aunt Vivian's. That part of me seemed set on automatic pilot. I hardly saw Jen, except for classes and morning break.

Deena was in a snit about having to transfer to another school, and seemed to be going out of her way to be difficult. We argued about what colour wallpaper to put up in our new bedroom. We argued about what we were going to eat for supper, who would fix it and who'd clean up afterwards. I gave up trying to make her pick up her dirty clothes. Without Mom around, Deena vegetated in front of the TV or sprawled out listening to her radio. If she had homework, I never saw it. And it was almost impossible to get near the phone. I hated to bother Mom about it because when she finally got home, she was too tired to do anything but collapse and put her feet up for a few minutes before running a hot bath and falling into bed.

By the time our next Youth Orchestra practice came around, I was clumsy with nervousness. As I stood waiting for the bus after school, I was tempted to forget it and go for a walk along the breakwater, study for my French test, vacuum the apartment — anything but face Maestro Hoffmann and risk further humiliation. Not that it could ever be as bad as last time. After a week's work I could feel the strength returning to my lip muscles. The tricky Beethoven passages were under control, memorized.

Hilary caught my arm as I walked into the rehearsal hall. "Sammie, were you able to practise?"

"I got double duty," I said, trying to laugh off my jitters. "I practised every lunch hour, and then I went to my aunt's after school. I had to practise in my uncle's workshop — with his tools and some fishnets that need repairing."

Renée's nose crinkled. "Smelly, eh?"

I shivered at the memory. "Actually, no, but I half froze. There was only a small electric heater in there."

Maestro was heading toward the podium. Tension coiled inside me at the sight of his slim, controlled bearing. I turned away with a feeling almost like hatred.

Hilary patted my shoulder. "You'll do fine, Sammie, I know you will. Are you still coming over? My family's looking forward to meeting you."

I smiled weakly and sat down. Julie wasn't here yet, which was unusual. Most days she was warming up by the time I came in, her sleek dark hair dancing as she nestled her violin on her shoulder.

"Hi." Arthur joined me. "So we get to face the executioner again, eh?"

"Yeah." Nervously I blew into my horn. "I got in ten hours of practice, so maybe I'll do okay. How about you?"

He whistled. "I only did three."

In front of us Amy was giggling at something Ian McCall, the principal bassoon player, had said.

Julie swept in at the very last minute. I could tell just by looking at her that something was terribly wrong. Her face was pinched and pale. I tried catching her eye, but she sat looking straight ahead as if something on Maestro's music stand was vitally important. She didn't even scoot her chair away from Geoff Harris-Hughes.

Maestro rapped his baton. "Get out the Beethoven," he said curtly once we'd warmed up with the D major and minor scales. When we came to the tricky passage, he stopped us cold. "French horns. Do you know it?"

It felt like war. Beside me, Troy, Jason and Arthur were tense with determination. We slugged the part out, challenging him to tear us down the way he'd done a week ago.

He didn't. He frowned. "Do it again." We did. At last he barked out, "Letter B. Violins and woodwinds, bring it in *leggiero* and then we build, build, *crescendo*, expand, until the horns enter *sfor-zando*." He scowled at us and gave the upbeat.

I was exhausted when rehearsal ended. At least there'd been no mistakes Maestro could pin on me. This time most of his nagging had been aimed at the violas. I sat there, horn in my lap, as the guys packed up. Maestro flitted around the room like a wasp at a picnic.

Arthur grinned at me. "Maybe you're off the hook."

"Wouldn't count on it," Jason muttered. "That man never forgets anything."

Julie was heading toward me. Even after more than an hour of playing, her face was still tight. "Sammie — "

"Samantha!" Maestro pounced. "I will listen to you now, in my office."

Helplessly I shrugged at Julie. When Maestro gave orders, it didn't pay to make him wait.

I felt trapped in the small room filled with trophies and filing cabinets. My hands shook as I adjusted the music stand in front of me.

For an ominous moment Maestro was silent. I squirmed in my seat, burning under his scrutiny. "I hadn't realized your difficulties," he said in a dry, precise voice. "Another player took the trouble to inform me. Perhaps I was unduly harsh."

"It got worked out," I said in a hurry. Maestro's intensity crowded in on me until I felt like a specimen under a microscope. Was this how court musicians felt centuries ago, when they risked losing their heads to irate kings? I took control of myself and played.

"Much better," he conceded. "I dare say next time you won't let as much time pass if you have similar problems?"

"No," I mumbled. Heat flooded my face, probably turning it the same colour as the brilliant fuchsia poster near the door.

"It takes a great deal of dedication to become a musician," he said. "Equally so, to *remain* one. The simplest passage demands exquisite control, the deepest understanding. In the arts we cannot be satisfied with the known, but rather, must stretch to seek new vision." Maestro smiled at me so unexpectedly that tears sprang into my eyes. "Keep working, Samantha," he said. "Someday you will be a fine musician. Come to me if you have problems. I will help if I possibly can. See you next week."

I thanked him and walked out in a daze.

Julie rushed toward me. Her eyes were electric with emotion. "Sammie — "

But Hilary and her father reached me first. "How'd it go?" Hilary asked.

"Okay." I looked at Julie, trying to include her.

Mr. Wong gave me a warm smile. "That's good. Shall we go now?"

"Call me," Julie said tersely. "It's crucial."

I promised, and followed Hilary and her father.

A whole range of impressions lingered after my visit with the Wong family. A cluster of curious, dark-eyed children, one brave enough to announce that he was learning violin. A grey-haired grandmother who spoke little English. A lovely aroma coming from the kitchen. And the kind of calm atmosphere that went with orderly discipline and plenty of love.

I felt calmed as the elevator carried me up to the apartment. When I unlocked the door, I found the living room dark. Only the kitchen light was on.

"Where've you *been*?" Deena's petulant voice came from the darkest part of the room.

I turned on a lamp. She was slumped in the reclining chair, her eyes puffy and red. "At Hilary's," I said. "I told you, she invited me over to practise and have supper after orchestra."

Deena sat up straighter. "You never told me! You never told me *anything*."

I sighed and set my horn down. My music folder and purse slumped to the floor. "I told you. You were stuffing your face in front of the TV — with *my* chocolate chip cookies." I was positive I'd told her. I'd been so mad because she'd dug in without asking, and it was about time she started helping around the place.

"You did not." Deena's voice rose. She kicked at the chair. "Suppertime comes, and nobody's here. What'm I supposed to do, eat out of a can?"

"It wouldn't hurt." I glared at the messy apartment. "When *I* cook, no, you can't be bothered — you say you're not hungry. Because you've been gobbling down all the sweet stuff in the house. Why should I try to be Mom all the time? You even expect me to pick up your filthy clothes and wash them. I've got my own problems to worry about."

"So?" she said sullenly. "You're older. You have to take care of me."

"Oh get real!" I yelled at her. "How can I do that if you won't even listen? I'm telling Mom, and she'll make you stay with Aunt Vivian, I bet."

Deena's cheeks flamed. She lurched out of the chair, with angry tears glistening in her eyes. "Try and get rid of me, eh? All you do is nag, nag, nag, and make it obvious I'm just a pain."

Next door the volume of the Wallaces' TV went up. I grabbed my music folder and threw it. Sheets of Beethoven, Corelli, Tchaikovsky, Copland and Alexina Louie scattered across the room. Damned neighbours, damned apartment, damned — "Oh what's the use," I muttered. "It's not like you even *try* to keep up your end of the deal." I wished Mom had never thought about buying a house. It was just too hard, having her gone all the time. I sighed. "Did you have anything to eat?"

"A peanut butter sandwich," Deena said sullenly. "The jam's all gone. And the honey too."

I sighed and bent over to pick up my music. The phone rang. Deena brushed roughly against me as she went to answer it.

"It's for you." Her voice was hostile. "Julie somebody. She's only called a million times."

Something clutched at my insides. "Hello?"

"Sammie." Julie sounded tense. "Can I come over?"

"Uh . . ." I looked around. The apartment looked awful, and I wouldn't be able to offer her anything — not unless she was crazy about peanut butter on bread crusts, or tinned beans. And I sure didn't want to show her my slob of a sister.

"I need to talk to you. I can't on the phone." There was an odd, hunted quality in her voice. I thought of Hilary's calm household and wondered if Julie was missing out on some of the same things I was, only for different reasons.

"Sure, okay," I said in a hurry. I glared at Deena, who gave me an insolent look.

The buzzer sounded forty minutes later. I pushed the button to unlock the outside door and waited nervously. Julie Blaustein was probably the richest kid in Port Salish if her dad owned the Haida Court mall. What would she think of our crummy apartment? I'd done a rushed cleanup, but even so the place looked tacky.

The minute Julie walked in, it was obvious she wasn't going to notice things like gunk crusted around the stove burners. Her face was tight, all flat planes and sharp angles. "Sammie, something awful has happened."

I shot Deena a lethal look, but she ignored me and plopped down in the recliner. *"Deena,"* I said through gritted teeth.

"What?" my sister asked, all innocence.

"Get lost," I said.

"Okay." She headed toward the front door.

"Deena! Cut it out."

"I'm doing what you said," she retorted. "You said get lost."

Hot anger flooded my face. How could my sister

be such a brat in front of Julie? "If you go out that door," I said, "I'm calling Aunt Vivian."

"Bully." My sister flounced past us to the bedroom.

Julie settled on the couch.

I sat down on the footstool and rubbed my fingers over the rattan weave. "What happened?" I asked.

Julie's foot was tapping impatiently. "Maestro told me — you know he's been going to see Matt every week . . ."

I hadn't known. Until today I'd had no idea our fierce, dictatorial director had it in him to be kind.

"Maestro said," Julie continued in a low, dull voice, "that Matt tried to kill himself."

The whole room seemed to lurch. A gaping blackness snatched away my breath. A thin film of hot sweat sprang out all over me, while my insides froze. I heard a gasp that must have been mine, but I felt so disjointed I wasn't sure.

"He said . . . he said . . ." Julie's voice cracked and suddenly she was shuddering. "He said Matt took his wheelchair down a flight of stairs."

"Oh God!" Images exploded in my mind. The hospital stairs were concrete. Sharp, unyielding ridges. It was probably twelve steps between landings; would that be enough to kill a person? If he didn't buckle himself into his chair . . . If he built up enough momentum . . . The clatter of a wheelchair out of control. The heavy thud of a flying body. Would he still be in his cast? I squeezed my eyes shut, but that didn't turn off my mind. "Is he all right?" I asked.

"Maestro said he had a slight concussion. And he broke his leg," Julie added with a bitter laugh. "Figures. He cracked the body cast, but it was almost time for it to come off, anyhow. Stupid idiot! He could've broken his neck."

I shuddered. That was probably what he'd been trying to do.

"Sammie, you've got to help." Julie's voice tugged at me.

I sat there with my chin in both hands, elbows digging into my knees. "What can *I* do? I'm not important to him."

"You went to see him. Several times. He'll know you care. As a person."

Julie was looking at me so intently I felt cornered. "Why don't *you* go?" I said. "You know him better than I do." How could I possibly face Matt now? What would we talk about? The weather? Beethoven?

"I can't." Dry, choking sobs burst out of her.

I didn't know what to say. I sat there and waited, feeling incredibly embarrassed.

"I can't," she said again. "I — we — once — "

And then I understood. "Oh Julie," I said, and went to sit beside her. "It must be awful."

"My damn *mother*!" she spat out. "She has to wreck everything. Matt was the best thing that ever happened to me, but no, she absolutely would not have it; *her* daughter was going to Europe to study; she was *not* to mix with 'common' young men. So she starts in on Matt and keeps at it until he hates anything connected with the name Blaustein. And then he gets tangled up with that bitch Amy. All she ever did was hurt him."

Julie was quivering. Tears pooled in my throat. I put my arm around her, the way Jen or Hilary would, but Julie acted like someone who wasn't used to being hugged. She just sat there, trembling. "I'm okay," she said after a few minutes, and blew her nose. "It's a lost cause, I know — I mean, Matt and me. But if you can help him in any way, I'll — I'll — "

A rush of emotion overwhelmed me. "I'll go," I promised. "I'll do whatever I can."

Julie's arms went around me in a convulsive hug. Just as quickly she was on her feet. "I have to go," she said. "They think I'm studying." And she dashed out, leaving me staring.

A few minutes later a faint shuffling sound caught my attention. Deena was standing there. "I guess I've been kinda bad," she mumbled. "Sorry."

Tears filled my eyes all over again. "Maybe I haven't been so great, either."

"Want to make some popcorn? I'm starved."

It sounded like a good idea. On our way to the kitchen I shoved against my sister. She shoved back. And then, like when we were little kids, we stood there nose-to-nose, seeing who'd be first to stare the other down.

Eleven

*I*t was easier to promise to go see Matt than figure out the best way to do it. I couldn't just innocently walk in and say hi. Several days passed. Jen kept asking what was bugging me, but I couldn't tell her. I kept thinking of Julie's anguished face. I couldn't betray her, even though I knew Jen would be sympathetic.

More time passed. Julie called and I felt like real scum when I had nothing to tell her. "Maestro keeps phoning," she said. "He asks if I've been to see Matt, and . . ." Her voice wavered. "It's *urgent*, Sammie."

I knew that. But Deena was dancing in front of the TV, distracting me. And Mom was due home in half an hour. "I'll see him before our next practice," I promised.

"Promise?"

The lonely, uncertain sound in Julie's voice was unsettling. I wished she'd go back to being her crazy, off-the-wall self. I also wished she'd hang up and leave me alone. "I promise."

"Thanks," she said after a slight hesitation. "You're a real friend, Sammie. I'll never forget this."

I took a deep breath and swung the telephone cord. "People helped us a lot when my dad was sick. Now I guess it's my turn."

That didn't make the prospect of another hospital visit any easier. I broke down and told Jennifer. I asked Glenna if she had any ideas. Nothing came of it.

Wednesday after school I sat shivering in Uncle Amos's workshop. I was sick and tired of facing Aunt Vivian and sometimes Blake every day. My aunt never forgot to let me know she was doing me a favour. And she'd started asking awkward questions about why Mom hadn't been home the last few evenings she'd called. I wondered if Uncle Amos had told her the news yet.

I glared at the heap of fishnet waiting in the corner to be repaired. I glared at Uncle Amos's mechanical gadgets sitting in pigeonholes on a shelving unit. Not that I was mad at Uncle Amos. After all, he'd loaned Mom money for the house. He was quiet, maybe even shy, and seldom home. Too bad I couldn't send Aunt Vivian and Blake out to sea with him.

I was sick of practising in my jacket and gloves. What did Aunt Vivian think she was doing, anyhow? "Come over here and practise, dear. Practise and freeze. And be grateful." I blew a long blatty tone through my horn. It bellowed out like a sick walrus. Some of Uncle Amos's tools rattled in sympathy. I stood up and held my horn out like a hunting horn, blew another blast, then another. A wild craziness seized me. I tried playing an elephant call. Not bad. I did a cow. I put my hand back in the bell of my horn and tried doing the foghorns. After several attempts I was almost satisfied. In my mind I could see myself standing out on Tillicum Point in the fog — not that I'd be heard over the rumble of a ship's engine.

I shook myself and started belting out Deena's favourite Colin James song, full blast.

Without warning a tomato splatted on the cement floor near my feet. As I looked up an egg came hurtling right at me. I ducked. It smashed against a gasoline can. "Blake," I said, "you're a real jerk, you know that?"

My cousin stood, sneering, in the doorway, wearing his usual case of acne. He replied with an obscene gesture.

My insides knotted. Blake, at fifteen, was bigger than I was. If I ever let it slip that he frightened me, I'd be lost. "Same to you," I said, and waited for him to leave.

He didn't. Instead, he sauntered into the workshop. "Let me see the horn," he said.

I tucked my French horn tighter beneath my arm, but Blake grabbed the coiled tubing and yanked it away. *"Blake!"* I yelled. "Give it back! If you so much as dent my horn I'll kick you where it really matters."

With a grin, my beast of a cousin put the mouth-piece to his lips and sent hideous sucking, kissing sounds through my horn.

I sighed. Now I'd have to boil my mouthpiece before I played again. "Beautiful, Blake," I said. "Almost as great as your violin playing." And then the idea hit. It was preposterous. It was totally unreal. And I had no idea if I could pull it off. "Where *is* your violin, by the way? I haven't seen it for a long time." I tried to keep my voice casual, but excitement fizzed inside me like a shaken pop bottle.

"Closet." He went back to his gross sounds, then started swivelling his hips like a pervert.

"Oh get out of here," I muttered. "Your mom'll hear and then she'll know just how sick you really are."

"She's shopping," Blake retorted.

I did not like the idea of being there alone with my cousin. On the other hand, it was a green light for my idea. "Can I borrow your violin?" I asked.

"What for?" he asked suspiciously.

"A good cause."

"What's in it for me?"

I drew in a steadying breath and tried not to look at the large white pimple on his nose. "Five bucks?"

Blake's small pig eyes studied me. "Gimme ten and it's yours."

"Oh come on! What are you, the Mafia?" I only had twelve dollars in my purse. If I gave Blake ten, it would mean peanut butter sandwiches and milk in a Thermos for lunch every day.

"Ten bucks. That is, if you want my violin *plus* your precious French kissin' horn back all nice and shiny like it is right now."

"That's extortion!"

"It was your idea," he said. "Well? I can't wait all day."

I wished Julie were with me. She'd know how to rupture my cousin's enormous ego. I picked up the half-squished tomato. "My horn first. Or no deal."

"Ten bucks?"

I sighed. "Yes, Blake." I hoped Julie would be satisfied. If it happened to make a difference for Matt, it would be worth far more than ten dollars.

Blake's bedroom was awful. The closed curtains allowed little light to enter, and the overhead fixture was covered with stickers. Rumpled sheets trailed from the bed into a tangle of clothes on the floor. The walls were filled with posters of nude women and racing cars, and the mirror had horrible squirmy words written on it with black marker. I stood halfway between Blake's closet and the door, wishing I'd never thought of the violin. Didn't Aunt Vivian *know*?

The closet, naturally, was packed from floor to ceiling. As Blake began tossing things out, I was tempted to put on the cleated hiking boots that flew past me and deliver a good kick to the seat of his grey jogging pants.

"How come you need it now?" he asked when the closet was half emptied. "I gotta meet somebody."

"The deal's off if your mom gets home before you hand me the violin," I warned.

Blake grunted and flung a mouldy sweatshirt across the room. "I bet your mom just loves doing your laundry," I said.

A ratty grade nine math book grazed my left ear, followed by some very explicit photographs that made my insides shudder.

The violin was at the bottom of the closet under a heap of crumpled dress shirts, along with a half-petrified banana peel, a crusty gym sock and a leaking bottle of after-shave.

"And now the ten." Blake crowded in on me.

"Does your mom know what you've got in here?" I demanded, trying to regain the upper hand.

Blake sneered. "Wouldn't you like to know. I bet your little sister would *love* to get her hands on it."

"Shut up!"

Blake leaned closer. "You know what I mean. The kid's begging for it every time I see her."

"You filthy rat!" Biting ants seemed to be swarming all over me. My hand shot out and smacked him across the cheek. "I bet your room's crawling with bugs. *Besides* the big roach with zits all over its face." I flung two five dollar bills on top of the pile of junk and turned to go.

Blake had gone a dull red. "You better shut up if you wanna get outta here alive."

I decided it was time I told Aunt Vivian I wouldn't be coming to practise anymore. Halfway to the bus stop I went into a convenience store to phone Deena and say I'd be late.

Twelve

*T*here was plenty of time before the bus came. I felt as nervous as I had playing in front of Maestro. The whole plan depended on how convincingly I could lie.

Fortunately nobody else was at the bus stop. Ignoring a paper boy and a couple of kids who were fooling around on bikes, I set my horn beside the bench and opened the violin case. A musty smell wafted out. I shuddered, half expecting to see cockroaches skittering for cover. An enormous wad of dried gum was cemented to the green lining. And the poor violin looked as though Blake had tried skateboarding on it.

There'd be no problem getting Matt to believe the instrument needed repair. The bow was half-bald. Stubs of broken horsehair protruded from the tip and the frog. Remembering some of Blake's tricks to avoid practising, I turned one of the tuning pegs. It protested with a stiff creak but finally gave.

I loosened it until the D string came free in large rounded curves, then fell away with a metallic slither. Perfect.

A bus came. I slapped the case shut and lugged both instruments on board, asking for a transfer. And wondered about Matt.

When I walked onto the eighth floor, I saw the nurse who'd been so angry the day Matt fell. She recognized me. "In to see Matt?" she asked, almost friendly. "He could really use some company."

I felt like a total nerd, with two instruments. In a hurry I asked when Matt would be transferred to rehab.

The nurse stood there, hands in her pockets. "It's hard to say, now, with his leg in a cast. He was supposed to have gone this week."

Matt's room was even darker than Blake's. The drapes were pulled, the lights off. The TV screen was blank. The once cheery poinsettia drooped, leaves yellowed and sickly. And Matt lay there motionless, covers up to his chin. His hair was dirty and had grown so long he looked like a street kid, maybe an addict, rather than a talented musician.

Tears sprang into my eyes. How could I play games with Blake's violin in this dreary room? It was immoral, playing on Matt's emotions at such a critical time. Then I saw the monkey, perched on the paper towel dispenser, cocky as ever. "Hi, Matt," I said.

"Get lost, Sam," he said in a lifeless voice.

He's depressed, I reminded myself. *He feels like*

there's no reason to keep on living. I swallowed hard and tried not to stare at the large bruise that mottled Matt's forehead — at least the part of it that was visible through his stringy, unkempt hair. The tube no longer dangled from his nose, but he was still terribly thin. "Sorry to hear about your accident," I mumbled.

He turned away.

I sat in a green vinyl chair.

"Get lost, Sam."

I thought of Julie's anguished face. For her sake, I couldn't let Matt get rid of me so easily. "The name's Sammie," I muttered. "Or Samantha, if you must." I kicked the chair legs and then remembered that Matt's legs could no longer kick.

Matt said nothing. Neither did I. I sat there and waited. And waited. At the far end of the hall I could hear the clatter of dinner carts.

Without warning, running feet pounded past. The intercom blazed to life. "Doctor 99 to 838; Doctor 99 to 838."

Electric currents sizzled through me. My heart thudded out of control, and it was hard to breathe.

"Doctor 99 to 838." More running feet. And then an impossible prickly silence.

"God, oh God." My voice was working and I'd hardly realized it, while my hands squeezed the metal chair arms so hard they bent slightly.

"Somebody's dying." Matt's voice sounded squeezed, too.

My teeth chattered. "I know. They ran like that when my dad — " Only there hadn't been a call for

Doctor 99. That was the emergency code. Dad's death had been expected.

At last Matt looked at me. "838 had surgery this morning."

"God." My teeth chattered harder. I doubled my knees to my chest and wrapped my arms around them, but that did nothing to stop the shivering.

"Here," Matt said after a long silence. He tugged at his top blanket and awkwardly handed it to me.

"Thanks." Feeling strange and light-headed, I draped it over my head like a shawl. The warmth from the blanket seemed far away at first, but gradually it began seeping into me.

Dinner arrived, but Matt wouldn't let the kitchen girl turn on the lights. He didn't touch his meal. The room grew darker and darker. The sun must have set. A while later I heard someone in the hallway closing all the doors.

"838's gone." Matt's voice was hoarse. "They're taking the body to the morgue."

All over again I began shuddering. This was what Matt had in mind for himself just last week. I was afraid to look at him, though it was the warmth from his body that had helped pull me out of shock. I heard a gurney being wheeled past, accompanied by quiet footsteps. I wondered who the patient had been and what had gone wrong.

"You brought a violin." Matt sounded as though he were forcing himself to change the subject. "What's it for?"

Heat flooded my face. "It's my cousin's," I stammered, wanting to escape. But Matt was talking to me for a change, so I couldn't back out. In the dim light I could no longer see the coloured speckles in the carpet. Matt was little more than a shadow in his bed. "It's in terrible condition," I added.

"What's that got to do with me?"

"Nothing. I was just on my way home from practising at my aunt's." I squirmed in my chair and folded the blanket.

"Practising . . . violin?" he asked.

"No. It was just a dumb, stupid idea. I'd better get going. My sister's home alone." But I didn't get up.

Matt sighed. "So you wanted me to have a look at it. Okay, let's see if it's in such bad shape." His thin arm reached up to pull the light cord at the head of the bed.

I blinked as a fluorescent glow flickered in the ceiling. My hands trembled when I gave Matt the violin.

He opened the case and snorted with derision. "Where'd they get this, the dump?"

"Pawn shop, I think. My cousin was pretty hard on it."

Matt held the violin up, studying its curves, running a finger over the wood. Anger flared in his face. "This thing is a total wreck. How could any parent let a kid abuse a musical instrument so badly?"

I looked at the floor and mumbled something about Blake.

"Looks like he left it out in the rain — or worse."

Matt pointed. "See how it's cracked? It'll have to be glued in several places. And it sure wouldn't hurt to get it refinished." He frowned at the bow. "Needs rehairing, but it probably wouldn't be worth it — it's too warped."

I watched Matt's face. This was the first time I'd seen him show interest in anything since the wreck — except for getting up off the floor the last time I'd been in.

He looked at me. "What's all this for, anyhow? What do you need to know?"

I felt as though my chair had dematerialized. "It's — " Frantically I tried to rearrange bits of the story I'd planned. If Matt found out it was all a plot to cheer him up, he might end up worse than before. "My aunt — " I shook myself and tried to think clearly. I'd always hated phonies, and here I was, lying. "She wants to sell it," I stammered. "My cousin quit lessons a long time ago, and I said I'd ask around to see if it was worth anything, and where she could get it fixed." I studied my fingernails and hoped Matt would believe me.

"It's not even worth two bucks like this," he scoffed. "I could give you the names of some good repairmen, but they'll really tell your aunt a thing or two when she takes it in." With the bow he began jabbing at the gum stuck to the case.

I drew in a long breath. "I was afraid of that," I said, trying to sound disappointed. I reached for the violin. "Thanks anyway, Matt."

"Wait a sec," he said. "Hand me a towel, and I'll get it looking a bit more respectable."

I did, and watched silently as he loosened the strings, then carefully polished the wood. Blackish smudges mottled the white terry towel. After a while the few unscratched surfaces almost began to gleam. "Were you the one who brought the monkey?" he asked under his breath as he rubbed at a spot by the bridge.

Heat boiled into my face. "Some of us . . . thought it was kinda cute," I mumbled. I didn't dare mention Julie. "Sorry."

Matt ignored me and went to work tightening the strings. But it was obviously difficult for him to tune the instrument while lying down. He swore and raised the head of his bed. Pillows cascaded to the floor. While I picked them up, Matt grabbed the hoist dangling above him and pulled himself up straighter. He tucked the violin beneath his chin. His hands shook as he drew the bow across the strings.

His pale fingers moved on the fingerboard, long and slim, almost aristocratic. With the violin on his shoulder Matt seemed to go into a trance. A burst of music drowned out all the hospital sounds. It was from the final movement of the Beethoven violin concerto, which we'd begun learning last fall. I'd heard Matt do better plenty of times, but probably Blake's violin was partly to blame. The door opened, just a crack, and astonished faces peered through, listening.

But before Matt had played very much, his hands began trembling so violently they gave Beethoven the hiccups. Suddenly Matt's face was twisting into odd spasms. Without warning the violin clattered between the bed rails.

I grabbed it just in time and sat there speechless. Matt Bruckner was crying.

"Sounded good, Matt," said a voice in the hallway.

"Get the bloody hell out of here!" he screamed.

The nurses vanished.

I hesitated.

"What's the matter with you, Sam?" he raged. "I said, *get out*. Are you going deaf or something? A deaf musician — what a laugh."

"Not if you happen to be Beethoven," I said, and then bit my lip.

Matt moaned and began crying like a little kid.

My heart hammered. My stomach felt full of earthworms. I got up and closed the door, then returned to the chair at Matt's bedside. "I'm sorry," I mumbled. There just wasn't anything better to say.

"Get out!" he yelled, then swore. "Who ever gave you the right to come in and start messing with my life?"

Tears smarted in my eyes. I put Blake's violin back into the case, but the bow was on the other side of Matt's bed. I reached for it. "I sort of know how it feels, that's all."

The words he flung at me were some of the same ones he'd used the night we came to play Christmas carols. Hot shame rushed to my face. I packed the violin away and promptly tripped over my French horn.

Useless. Totally useless. Hating myself, I got to my feet. Matt no longer seemed aware of me. Raw wailing sounds were coming from deep inside him, reminding me of times I'd heard Mom crying soon after Dad died. There was no way I could leave him feeling like that.

Nervously I climbed over the rails and sat on his bed, beside his paralyzed legs, which stretched out like a couple of counterfeit bills. The leg cast was a hard outline beneath the covers. I put my hand on his shoulder.

He recoiled into a mass of quivering sinews. There wasn't much else left of him.

It was like being slammed in the stomach by a city bus. "Sorry," I mumbled, and pulled away.

His claw-like fingers seized my wrist before I had a chance to get down. "Don't go." He hiccupped.

I almost giggled from nervousness. I wanted to cry, too. Instead, I put my arms around him and held his head against me, willing comfort into him. He slumped and cried. I held him for a long time, thinking about his losses, about mine, and wishing I could stamp out the awful pain that was tearing him to pieces, show him some good reasons to keep on living. I thought about Dad, about Mom, and Deena. About Glenna. And Matt's family too, whoever they were. I thought of Julie and Jen, even Amy. But always my mind came back to Matt.

Much later he began to speak, incoherently at first, about his sister. It was a long time before he relaxed. When I mentioned seeing Tamara's grave, fresh tears streaked down his face, but soon afterwards he fell asleep nestled against my shoulder.

Hardly daring to breathe, I got up and carefully lowered the head of his bed. Matt stirred once and I froze, but he didn't awaken. Sleeping, his face was open and vulnerable, so different from the face I'd seen when I first came in. I tucked the covers around him and tiptoed out with my horn and Blake's violin.

Julie and a middle-aged woman were waiting in the hallway.

"Oh Sammie," Julie said. Her green eyes were bright with tears but she looked steadily at me.

"I — " There wasn't anything I could say.

The woman had a kind, motherly face, and soft dark hair that was streaked with grey. Her warm brown eyes glistened above wet cheeks. "Bless you, Sammie," she said in an emotion-choked voice. She reached for my hand and clasped it for a moment, then slipped into Matt's room.

"Who's that?" I asked, staring at the closed door.

"His mom." Julie picked up my horn. "I'll carry this."

"No, you don't have — "

"You've just worked a miracle, Sammie Franklin." Julie's voice wobbled as she walked close beside me, carrying my French horn. "That kid's been keeping everything inside ever since the wreck. He's always been like that — too hard on himself, has to be perfect. It could've killed him."

I shuddered.

"But," Julie went on, chin slightly higher, "it

looks like you helped him realize it's okay to be human." She sniffled. "Okay to . . . cry."

Everything blurred as we walked along the corridor. Every now and then Julie's shoulder brushed against mine. There were no words to express the currents of emotion that linked us.

One other thing was very clear. Dad's presence shimmered all around, bathing me in that same overwhelming love that had surrounded me on Christmas Day.

Thirteen

*T*he anniversary of Dad's death came soon after that.

Mom had to rush to get to work that day, so not much was said at breakfast. Jen didn't remember any particular significance about the twenty-sixth of January, and I didn't really want to bring it up. All day I carried around a dull heaviness that dragged me down like a dismal rain. The last thing I wanted was to go home and face Deena and her friend Karla. Most likely they'd be pigging out and leaving their garbage all over the apartment.

Late-afternoon sunlight slanted through bare oak branches. In only an hour or so the short winter day would fade to dusk. Instead of catching the bus home, I walked several blocks farther and boarded the Blevins Point bus. As houses and yards slipped past, I pulled my French horn into my lap and rested my chin on the heavy black case.

Dad seemed so far away. I tried to visualize his

face, to imagine a conversation. It had been easy to do in the first few months after his death, but now the images were stale and false.

The sun glanced off water as the bus rounded a bend, revealing the strait. Off to the left dedicated golfers were going through their ritual in spite of the cold. I pulled the cord when I saw the familiar stone wall of the cemetery.

The grounds were quiet. The distance on foot to Dad's grave seemed interminable. Suddenly I wondered if I should have come so late in the day. The gates closed in just half an hour, and the buses might not run very often this far out of town.

I cut through the wooded fringe area, ducking beneath low branches. Needles and fallen twigs crackled under my feet and the air was thick with the smell of leaf mould. Startled crows flapped away, cawing, over the symmetrical rows of grave-stones. Already a creamy light was spilling through the sky. The trees cast long shadows. I bent to pick up a few fallen cones.

I paused at Tamara Bruckner's grave, a bare mound where the dirt still hadn't settled. The mark-ings on the stone seemed cold and final. A lump swelled in my throat. With a prayer kind of feeling for Matt, I set one of the pinecones beside the vase where real crocuses, not plastic, bloomed.

One of the few cars in sight crawled along the laneway toward the gates. Farther away I could see workers tossing equipment into the back of a truck.

I walked quickly now in spite of the heavy weight of my horn. There was the familiar row of small firs. The slanting sunlight was yellow on the smooth granite. FRANKLIN. The lettering was clear and black. I set the remaining pinecones beside Dad's marker, then parked my horn case and sat on it.

"Dad," I said, testing the sound of my voice in the immense quiet surrounding me. The silence gulped it up, just as all these lives had been gulped up by the ultimate silence. "Dad, I miss you." My voice caught. There was no answer, no sense of loving warmth like the sudden rush that had enveloped me on Christmas Day or at the hospital, only stillness. I swallowed hard. "Dad, I love you." The lump in my throat became tears, which trickled down in chilly streaks. I licked the salt off my lips, blew my nose. "Dad, I wish you were still with us."

What would he have said? Probably something like "Me too," or "I didn't exactly have much choice about this." For an instant I could see the warm light of his brown eyes, the way he used to look at me when I'd done something nice.

My hands were red from the cold. I slipped them into my pockets and sat there, rocking my French horn case slightly. It was over. Life with Dad, but also Dad's suffering. Somehow we'd managed without the entire world falling apart. Facing the future was still scary. So was the *now*, with Mom working herself half to death and Deena getting out of control.

Loneliness chiselled through me. The wind probed my face, reaching for my neck. I wanted to cry, but that would be like giving up. *Courage*. It seemed as if Dad's voice was saying it, but probably that was just my imagination.

I sat there and hunched my shoulders. Another car went out the gate. The sky was a pale fish-belly colour; against it the trees stood in stark silhouettes. A tug of fear caught at me but I didn't want to leave yet. The noble thing would be to stay the night by Dad's grave, since obviously nobody else had been here. But it was just plain too cold, and I couldn't dump that kind of worry on Mom. In my imagination I saw newspaper headlines: Heartbroken Daughter Perishes during Nighttime Vigil at Father's Grave. That would get Deena thinking, all right. Maestro would be sorry about bullying me. Maybe Matt would notice and get his act together. But Jen would understand. Julie too.

The thought of Julie cheered me. For a long, intense moment I wished she were with me, with her crazy remarks that managed to say a whole lot. Dad flashed through my mind then, strong and vivid, and how proud he'd been of my playing.

Without really thinking it through, I knelt down and undid the latches on my horn case. The coiled tubing was frigid. I stood up and blew air through my horn, warming it. It was Mendelssohn that I played, soft and intense phrases from the "Nocturne" in *A Midsummer Night's Dream*. It seemed to fit. The quiet, sweet melody reached out over the cemetery, over the water, into the sunset. If Dad could hear, he would be pleased. If not, that was all right too.

The moon was rising. And suddenly a taxi

braked to a halt with the grate of tires on gravel. My mother got out. Her face looked tight, pinched.

"Mom!" I said. "I thought you had to work."

She bent and said something to the driver; then she joined me. The taxi waited, engine idling. "Oh Sammie." Mom sounded impossibly tired. "I'm so glad to see you."

"What about work?" I asked again.

She shook her head, then pulled a scarf around her neck. "I've got a horrible headache. The boss sent me home."

I was relieved to see her, in spite of the headache. "Did you want to be by yourself?" I asked awkwardly. She might want some privacy.

"No, that's all right." Mom rubbed her hands over her eyes. "We don't have much time, anyway. They were just about to lock the gates when I came in." She looked at my horn. "Playing?"

"Yeah, a little," I said, embarrassed. "It seemed — right, you know?"

My mother smiled wearily. "He would've liked that." Her eyes went watery.

I put my horn away and stepped back to walk past other markers. ARMBRUSTER. SCHULZ. NOHONIAK. FITZWILLIAM. Would Dad have liked the people who were buried beside him?

"Sammie?" Mom called. "It really is all right, love. I'd like your company."

She took my arm. I tried to imagine how she must feel, but it was hard to stretch beyond my own emotions. A few minutes later a pickup rattled over and honked. "We're closed," a worker called out.

"We're on our way," my mother replied. She gave my arm a little squeeze. Once in the taxi she rested her head against the back of the seat.

Worry gnawed at me. I wondered if she'd be able to hold up until our old house sold.

Fourteen

A couple of nights later I dreamed Matt was calling me. In the dream I was on Uncle Amos's fishboat, the *Ellen Marie*. Uncle Amos and the others had gone somewhere, leaving me alone on the water. The fog closed in around me, soft and quiet. I wasn't frightened, because the steady booming of the foghorns reassured me that I was in no danger. Then I heard Matt's voice. "Sammie? Sammie!" The call came from the open water. "I'm coming!" I shouted. I tried to turn the boat in that direction but I couldn't change its course. "Sammie! Sammie!" Matt's voice grew anguished, and fainter by the minute. "Matt!" I cried, and awakened with a jolt.

"Huh?" Deena mumbled. "You say something?" Then she turned over and went back to sleep.

I sat up in bed and huddled there in a shivering ball. The greenish numerals on the clock radio read 2:42. In the distance the foghorns called to one another. I went to the window and saw that all of Port Salish was fogged in, and even the hospital was only a glowing spectre in the mist. I gulped in a deep breath, praying that Matt was all right, and went to get a drink of water.

The living room light was on, making me wonder if I'd forgotten to turn it off when I went to bed. I went to see about it.

Mom sat in the recliner, wrapped in a quilt. She looked haggard. A mug was nearby on the coffee table.

"Mom?" I said hesitantly. "Are you all right?"

She gave me a strained smile. "I can't sleep."

"But Mom, you're so tired . . ." Not that lecturing would help her sleep; I knew that from my own experience. I crossed the room and sat on the footstool.

"It's idiotic, I know," Mom said ruefully, "but the minute I crawl into bed, I start worrying."

Sympathy rushed through me. "What are you worried about?" I tucked my cold feet inside the hem of my nightgown.

"Everything," she said with a defeated laugh. "I worry about whether I made the right decision with the house. I worry about the two of you. I worry about what would happen to you if anything happened to me."

"Oh Mom —" I got up and hugged her as if I were the parent and she the child. "Everything will be okay. Don't worry."

She gave me a squeeze, then let go. "I heard you call out in your sleep. Was it a bad dream?"

I sat back down on the stool, realizing suddenly that I'd never had the chance to tell her about my trip to the hospital with Blake's violin.

Mom's face softened as I told her. "I don't know what to do," I finished up. "He might never want to see me again. And I don't know what I'd say if I went back . . ."

Mom stood up. "Let's fix some hot chocolate." She picked up her mug and made a face. "Chamomile tea is supposed to work wonders for helping a person sleep, but it certainly doesn't do much good if you're feeling all shuddery. It's too thin."

We shared a companionable silence as we waited for our mugs to heat in the microwave. There was a thump in the apartment upstairs. And in the distance, the foghorns bellowed.

"It might be good if you went to see Matt again," Mom said slowly as she stirred powdered chocolate into the warm milk. "He surely must trust you by now. I imagine he could use a friend."

My first few sips of the hot creamy drink relaxed my still-shivery insides. "Something tells me I should go back," I said. "But I'm just . . . scared."

Mom's arm went around my shoulder. "I know how you feel. But you'll do fine. You're a kind person, Sammie. It rubs off on others."

I pulled back, embarrassed, and nearly choked on my hot chocolate.

Mom patted me on the back. "Are you all right?" Her concerned face no longer looked as worn.

"Yeah." I gave her a self-conscious grin. "How about you?"

"I'll live. In fact, I might even be able to sleep now."

* * *

School was dismissed early the next day because of a staff meeting. I backed away from Jen in the hallway, claiming Mom wanted me to pack things for moving, because I knew once we started talking the afternoon would slip by and I'd never get over to the hospital. An eerie superstition lingered, left over from my dream, but in the clear afternoon sunlight it was easier to convince myself I was just being silly.

I stopped by the apartment, where I dug out a Kleenex box full of chocolate chip cookies. I'd stashed it in the linen closet, since that was a place Deena rarely looked. I nibbled three and covered the rest with plastic wrap, hoping it wouldn't look too gross. Then I locked up and escaped before Deena arrived.

When I got to Matt's room, his bed was empty and the wheelchair was gone. A passing nurse told me he was in physiotherapy. I left a quick "Hello" scribbled on a paper towel and set the cookies beside it.

An aide came in just then to straighten the sheets. "Why don't you go down and see him in physio?" she suggested. "Visitors do that all the time, and with the little amount of company this guy gets, he'll be mad he missed you."

Somehow I doubted Matt would see things quite that way. "How's he been this past week?" I asked.

The woman's eyes were grey and calm. "Good, actually. Something seems to have changed his mind about a whole lot of things."

My heart fluttered. I took one backwards step toward the door, then another.

"You take the elevator all the way down to the basement," the aide called after me. "Then you hang a right. You can't miss it, with the signs."

I knew how to get there. I'd gone several times when Dad was down for treatments. My eyes smarted with unexpected tears. In its impassive way, the hospital was continuing with business as usual as if my father had never existed.

The scene was oddly familiar as I paused in the open doorway to the large physiotherapy area. To one side were curtained-off cubicles where patients received treatments like heat packs and massage. In the centre of the room a therapist was helping an elderly woman walk between a set of parallel bars. Here and there were various sets of apparatus which I'd never come to understand. Against one wall was a complicated set-up of pulleys and weights. Matt was laboriously transferring from a low table back into his wheelchair. He was using a sliding board to make the transfer easier, but even so it looked terribly hard with his leg extended in its cast.

As I watched, one end of the board slipped away from the table. I gasped. The therapist, a stocky woman, quickly caught Matt under his armpits and heaved him the rest of the way into his chair. "Why'd you have to go and break your leg?" she grumbled. "Weren't we offering enough in the way of entertainment?"

I shrank back. Matt wouldn't want me overhearing this conversation.

"May I help you?"

I jumped as another therapist stepped past me. "I came to see Matt Bruckner," I mumbled. "A nurse sent me down. But if he's busy . . ."

"Come on in." The young woman gave me a cheery smile and led me across the room. "Visitor for Matt," she announced.

By now he was sitting with his back to the pulleys and weights. He held the end of a strap in each hand and was methodically extending first one arm, then the other. As he did so, a weight rose and then slid back down in a column in the apparatus behind him.

"Sammie!" From his surprise, it was obvious Matt hadn't seen me peering in from the doorway. He stopped exercising, looking as though he didn't know what to say.

I didn't know what to say either. This version of Matt Bruckner was quite different. His hair was washed and trimmed so that it no longer fell into his eyes. He was wearing a Walkman headset, and his pyjamas were no longer stained and crumpled. Several autographs were scrawled across his cast. "A nurse sent me down here," I said, needing to explain. Groping for words, I read the names on his cast. They were all female. "So you've got a fan club, eh?" I said.

He gave me a rather twisted smile. "They're all captives, some of the nurses and the staff here in physio. If you sign, you'll be my first free convert from outside."

"Hey you over there!" called his therapist. "Don't get a swelled head just because of a little attention. Back to work!"

"Slave-driver," Matt muttered loudly enough for her to hear.

"That's what they all say," she retorted. "But if you want to get out of here you'd better mind."

"Slave-driver," he said again. He adjusted his headphones and went back to exercising with a vengeance. The equipment rattled. The weights rose to the top of their columns even more quickly than before.

The therapist stood back watching, a faint smile on her face. "I think it's time we added another kilogram."

Matt glowered at her. "I'm not going out for the Olympics."

"I'll be satisfied when you can lift your own weight in and out of that chair. Cast and all," she added pointedly.

He scowled at me. "It's your fault. If you hadn't come in, she never would've noticed."

A painful shyness washed over me. Matt's complaining was transparent enough; it would be obvious to anybody that he'd pulled out of that black depression. Yet I couldn't erase the memories of his sobbing, and holding him against me until his shuddering stopped.

"What are you listening to?" I stammered as the therapist did something to the weights.

Matt didn't quite meet my eyes. "Itzhak Perlman. Doing the Beethoven." He reached for the straps once more. "The violin concerto," he added, as if I might not know.

"Oh." Something quivered inside me. Maestro was forever reminding the violin section to listen to Perlman's recordings. He was supposed to be one of the best violinists in the world.

Matt worked the weights, this time stretching each arm toward the opposite knee and beyond. "I'd better get going," I said after a few minutes. "We're moving, and I have to pack."

He stopped again. "Where are you moving to?"

"Across town." I didn't want to admit we were moving to the Harbour District.

"Oh well," he said, as if that explained everything. "It won't be as hard as moving to Toronto or someplace."

I smiled and turned to go. Then my eyes fell on the signatures on his cast. "Should I sign it?" My voice sounded a little too jittery for comfort.

"Of course. What else is it good for? I can't exactly walk on it."

Again he wouldn't quite meet my eye, and I was afraid to look him directly in the face. Quickly I bent, fumbling in my purse for a felt marker, and wrote, "Good luck — Sammie," and the date in black. In a funny way the cool solid plaster felt more real than anything else on this whole visit.

* * *

"Sammie!" Deena hollered that evening, startling me out of *The Diviners*. We were supposed to read two chapters for literature in the morning, and I was so caught up in the book that I'd almost finished. "Telephone!"

"It's a guy," she added, not bothering to cover the receiver. "But don't be long, okay? Karla said Eric Wotherspoon told her he might call me, and I'll *die* if — "

I grabbed the phone, ignoring Deena as she prattled on. "Hello?" I said cautiously.

It was Matt. "The cookies are good," he said.

"Oh well . . . thanks." I stuck my little finger into the coils of telephone cord. Deena was lurking in the doorway. I glared at her and gestured for her to get lost. She didn't.

"My grandparents liked them too. My grandfather ate about five, and I couldn't even reach the box to put them away."

"Uh-oh." I wished I could quit shaking. I started wrapping the cord around my wrist. "Are there any left?"

"About half." His mournful tone made me smile. "And I can't reach them now either. When my grandparents left, they moved the table so they could get past."

"Uh-oh." I imagined how it must feel, being stuck in bed and unable to move far enough to reach a box of cookies. "Can you transfer into your chair and get them?"

"No. The chair's in the corner."

I relaxed a bit. "Call down to physio and get a cane."

There was a quick silence. "What do I need a cane for?" Now he sounded exasperated.

"To grab things with. You know, you can — "

"I get it. Not a bad idea." Pause. "Physio's closed until morning."

"Call a nurse then." The conversation was getting easier and easier. I unwrapped the cord from my wrist.

"No." Scorn rang in his voice and I smiled. "Oh well. The juice girl comes in twenty minutes. She'll have to move the table anyhow."

"Who is it?" Deena whispered.

"Just a sec," I said, and covered the receiver with my hand. "Get *lost*, Deena!" As usual she didn't, so I decided to try her trick. Stretching the telephone cord across the kitchen, I stepped into the broom closet and pulled the door shut. It was dark.

"Sorry," I said into the phone. "My sister was eavesdropping." Then, in the silence that followed, I wished I hadn't said anything.

"Thanks for the cookies, anyhow," Matt said.

"Well . . . that's okay." I squirmed restlessly and banged a broom handle. It clattered sideways, knocking against something else. A series of crashes and bangs erupted all around me.

"What was that?" Matt sounded stunned.

"I'm in the broom closet," I explained, trying to

keep the furious blush that was flooding my face from showing in my voice.

Matt started laughing. A sudden clunk, then another, jolted my eardrum, and then a thud.

"Matt?" I said hesitantly.

No answer, only more clunks. "I dropped the phone," he said sheepishly a moment later.

"Oh." I started laughing too.

"Who *was* that?" Deena demanded after we'd hung up. Her dark eyes sparkled with curiosity.

I wanted to yell at her, but I was still too cracked up to care. "Beethoven," I said, and went down the hall to our room.

Fifteen

*S*oon afterwards we got possession of the house and began moving our things. It was an incredible hassle with Mom gone so much, plus no car. By bus the trip took at least twenty minutes, and we couldn't carry much. Suddenly there was no time for anything but school and packing.

Jen borrowed her parents' station wagon one Saturday and came over to help. "I can't believe you guys lived here almost a year," she said, looking around the living room.

I dusted the china choirboys on the shelving unit and one by one, wrapped them in newspaper. The photo of Dad smiled at me from nearby. He'd given Mom a figurine for each birthday and Christmas, until they both decided she had enough. That was how they'd met, singing in the community choir.

"Should I take down the clock?" Jen asked.

I glanced at the antique-style wall clock. "Better

not. You could pack the books, though." It was hard to know what to pack, without Mom around to direct.

Jennifer began stacking books in piles around her. "*Shadow in Hawthorn Bay*," she murmured. "I loved that book. Oh! And you've got — " She glanced at me, holding a copy of *Whalesinger*. "Can I borrow this? It was never in the library when I wanted to check it out."

I had to smile. Ever since grade school Jen had spent half her time buried in a book. "Sure. That means one less to pack."

I packed Mom's delicate blown-glass vase, another gift from Dad, then sat on the floor with Jen. I put the biggest books in a separate box. The world atlas. The dictionary. *The Complete Works of Shakespeare*. The encyclopaedia set could wait. *A Practical Guide to Parenting* had several book marks sticking out. I opened it: How to Deal with Lying. That marker must've been for Deena. I closed the book, wondering how many markers had to do with her and how many with me.

"Oh, I remember this!" Jen was thumbing through a Dr. Seuss book that Deena and I had read over and over again.

I handed her another empty box. "We're packing, remember?"

Jen gave a dramatic sigh. "The sacrifices I make."

Deena and her friend Karla trooped in, giggling, their cheeks pink from the fresh air. "Got anything to eat?" Deena asked.

"Dry cereal," I said pointedly. "I thought you were going to pack, Deena."

"I am." Her voice was nonchalant. "I was just going to do my tapes and get started on clothes, right, Karla?" If Karla answered, it was muffled by the banging of cupboard doors. The two of them went down the hall with the box of Cheerios.

I sighed.

"Anthony does that all the time," Jen said. "Only he takes the toaster with him too, *and* half a loaf of bread."

It seemed ages since I'd been at the Cascardis' house. With Jen's four brothers and sisters underfoot we never had much privacy, but it was always a comfortable place. I felt as if I'd been drifting, somehow, ever since Dad's death. It was almost like being in the fog. Was I drifting away from Jen?

I shook myself. The living room looked bare with so many things packed away. "Bland," I said. "Mom called this place a rabbit cage once. Was she ever right!"

Jen laughed. "Don't we have a load already? I still haven't seen the inside of your new house, remember?"

"Deena!" I yelled. "We're going."

"Wait!" My sister emerged with a box of summer clothes, probably one that had been in our closet. "Here's some stuff. And I'll bring yours too."

Maybe my sister wasn't such a slob after all.

Jennifer and I stopped at our storage unit to pick up the bags of Dad's things from the hospital. Mom had given his clothes away long ago, donating them to a Third World relief organization, and these were just odds and ends. It was hard to imagine strange men wearing Dad's clothes in Latin America, maybe even Africa. In a way that made these black plastic bags all the more precious. Even the thought of a half-used can of shaving cream made me feel a little weepy.

Outside, it was sunny. The air almost smelled like spring.

Jen was an over-cautious driver. We crept along Qualicum Drive so slowly that people kept passing us. "This is weird," I said. "Almost like being on our own, know what I mean?"

"Let's get an apartment when we're in university," she said. "I'd give anything to get away from Anthony and Max."

I fidgeted with the radio. It was hard to think about another apartment right when we were moving out of one. "Could we afford it?"

"We could work," she said. "And it would be cheaper if we got another roommate."

We had to stop at the Fraser Street bridge. A boat was passing and the drawbridge was up. Jen giggled suddenly. "What would they do if fire trucks were on their way to a fire? Make the boat wait? Or what if you were walking across the bridge? Think there'd be time to get off before it went up?"

I'd wondered that myself. Soon the drawbridge would be part of my regular bus route to school. With luck, it wouldn't take any longer than from the apartment. I looked out at the loading docks, at the rust-coloured freight cars nearby. The water around one dock was filled with logs. Off to the left the afternoon ferry was on its way out of the harbour. I hadn't paid much attention to this part of Port Salish since I was a little kid. Would living nearby change anything?

The bridge came down and the light turned green. "Melanie had a party last night," Jennifer said abruptly. "Charmaine went with Adam. I didn't know if I should tell you."

For a moment I just looked at the old houses, at a laundromat, at a bowling alley. "Oh," I said.

Jen glanced sideways at me. "Are you okay? I mean, you've liked him such a long time."

How long had it been? Over a year. But somehow Adam had drifted off too. "It doesn't matter," I said.

"I was worried," she said. "But you seem . . . different. You're so tied up over that Matt guy. I thought maybe . . ."

Jen's voice sounded strained. Sadness caught at my throat. "It's no major crisis," I said. I hesitated, then barged ahead. "Am I a *lot* different?"

She gave me a smile that was somehow both apprehensive and relieved. "We're all changing — we can't stay kids forever." She parked in front of our new house.

The afternoon light was gentle on the peeling white paint. As we unloaded the boxes and garbage bags, Uncle Amos came around from the back, carrying a hammer.

"I've checked the steps," he said. "Tell your

mother the back should hold up for a while. I think you'll find the front solid now."

"Thanks." I smiled and reached for another box.

A smile flickered across my uncle's weathered face. "Here, I'll help you with those boxes." He tossed his tools into the back of his truck. He made several trips to the front steps and then was on his way.

Jen jabbed me with her elbow. "Who's that?" she whispered. "Has your mom got a boyfriend?"

"It's my uncle."

Jen's eyes widened. "You mean Blake's dad?" She giggled as the truck drove off. "He sure doesn't take after your uncle. How'd he get to be so — you know . . ."

"Natural inferiority." I didn't like remembering the time I'd slapped Blake, but then, I didn't like thinking about Blake under *any* circumstances. So far I hadn't figured out a way of returning his ratty old violin without having to face him or Aunt Vivian.

I went up the front steps cautiously, hating to step on the pale fresh boards Uncle Amos had hammered in. It was just like Uncle Amos to do something like that and then disappear. Waiting for Jennifer, I glanced at the damp flower beds. Green spikes were springing up. Daffodils, maybe? I'd have to tell Mom.

The living room was filled with sunlight. *"Oh,"* said Jen as we walked in. At first it was hard to tell if that was a good sign or bad. The faded wallpaper and worn carpet were all too obvious. But to me the place was beginning to feel like home. A few things were already in place — a calendar by the dead phone, a checkered tea towel hanging on a rack in the kitchen. When I opened the cupboards I found our best dishes, plus some canned goods.

"This is nice," Jen said in a hushed voice. "It feels *right*, know what I mean? Like lots of different people have lived here, and they all left part of themselves behind. Do I sound too weird?"

I laughed and set a box of books in the living room. "No." Actually, I knew what she meant. The house had its own personality, a friendly one. "Come on. I'll show you Deena's and my room, and I want you to tell me what we should do with it."

Jen stopped in the doorway. "It's so dark," she said.

"Yeah." I stood there looking at the gloomy old-fashioned wallpaper, tiny white flowers on a dark-green background. Even with sunlight beaming in I was tempted to turn on the light. "The room's great, except . . ."

"Strip the wallpaper," Jen suggested. "You have to do that, anyway, before you can paint it or put up new paper. It'd be easiest to do it before all your stuff's here." She inspected a seam. "I bet it'll peel."

I ran my thumbnail along the windowframe. The paper was a bit loose. Would Deena kill me? She hated the wallpaper too, but we were still arguing about what to do.

"Go on, try," Jen prompted.

With my thumbnail I picked at the paper, then pulled. A strip came away from the wall, leaving a pale streak the colour of newsprint. "I don't know . . ." A horrible guilty feeling nibbled at me. I'd ruined it, even before we moved in.

"Go on," said Jen. "Here, I'll help." A huge long strip pulled away in her hand, almost up to the ceiling. "This is easy. Sometimes Mom has to soak it first and then scrub like crazy."

I wanted to yell at her to stop, but with every strip she pulled, the room got brighter. It was incredible.

There was a sudden knocking at the front door. "Yoohoo, anybody home?" It was a woman's voice, not one I recognized.

"Pretend we're not here," Jen hissed. She peeked out the window.

The knocking came again. "Yoohoo!"

If it was one of our new neighbours, I didn't want to look like a snob. If it was somebody trying to sell vacuum cleaners, well, I'd send them away. I took a deep breath and went to answer the door.

A little woman with bright blue eyes grinned at me. Her short chalk-white hair shone like a cap above her lined face. "Hello," she said. "Are you the new folks? I've seen you coming and going, and then that man working here, so I thought I'd come and get acquainted. My name's Florence Crosbie, Flo for short, and I live next door, in the yellow house."

I mumbled my name and invited her in.

"I won't stay," she said. "I know you're busy."

Her keen eyes darted around the living room. "You'll like it here, I think — we have some nice people on this street. How many are there of you?" And then as Jen appeared in the doorway, "Are you two sisters?"

She seemed so genuinely interested that I relaxed. "We're friends," I said.

"And that man," Mrs. Crosbie continued, "he's your father?"

For a moment I wondered if she was snooping. But her lively eyes were direct and friendly. "That's my uncle," I said. "My father died last year."

Her face went sad. "Oh, what a shame. It's hard to lose your loved ones. I lost my husband ten years ago. Anyhow, I'm glad folks are looking out for you — that uncle of yours has been around quite often, checking the place over, fixing the fence, fixing the steps . . ."

For a moment I resented Mom's long work hours. She hadn't even let me know if it was safe to mention the house in front of Aunt Vivian.

"Anyway, I won't keep you." Mrs. Crosbie began backing up. Then she paused. "Franklin. You said your name was Franklin?" When I nodded, her forehead furrowed. "There were Franklins living a few blocks over until maybe twenty years ago. Though I don't suppose they would've been your people, it's a common name . . ."

I had a sudden dizzy sense, almost like balancing on a log bridge suspended over a rushing creek. "My father grew up around here," I said faintly.

Something inside me desperately wanted this woman to tell me she'd known Dad.

"I never knew them, myself," she said. "But Mr. Kirkpatrick down the street did, I think. I'll introduce you one day. I could show you the house — though it's other folks living there now, of course. Remember, now, if you need any help, don't hesitate to come and ask; I'm around most of the time."

Stunned, I thanked her.

"Does she ever *talk*!" Jen whispered once the front door closed.

"I like her," I said, and went to the uncurtained window. "She's nice." I looked out at the quiet street, with its old houses and shabby cars. Meeting people who'd known Dad when he was a kid — it was unbelievable, almost. I wondered how Mom would feel about it. For me, it seemed like a promise of answers to questions I hadn't known I'd asked.

Sixteen

"*S*ammie, I'd like you to pack the pots and pans, please" . . . "Sammie, you really should've come to the Smooth Dudes concert with us — it was awesome!" . . . "Don't forget, class, your essays on a Canadian poet are due next Wednesday, three pages minimum, and typed if possible."

Everywhere I went people were making demands. I couldn't begin to keep up with them. I felt trapped, like a slave. Deena was helping at home — sort of. I didn't dare push her or she'd stomp out and disappear for several hours. Meanwhile, Julie kept after me to go see Matt again. I felt guilty, especially since he'd gone to the trouble of phoning me that once. I couldn't work up the nerve to call him back, and besides, I just plain didn't have time.

Once Jen and I got the bedroom wallpaper stripped, Glenna took Deena and me shopping for paint and new paper. Deena did all right when we painted two walls, and she honestly tried with the wallpaper — sea gulls soaring in a misty blue. But she kept forgetting to make allowances for the pattern when she measured. After she ruined two strips, I got mad and she began to sulk. It wasn't much better when we put the paper up. No matter how hard we tried, Deena and I just couldn't work together.

It was a Friday afternoon. The only chance I'd had to relax all day was at lunch, with Jen. I had a headache, and cramps. And the weekend promised to be awful, with a hideous algebra assignment and a history test to study for — and our final moving day in just one week. Besides, Charmaine was having a party and I hadn't been invited. Now I was standing on the stepladder holding a long strip of dripping paper. I matched a gull's wing with the rest of its body on the adjacent strip and then carefully smoothed the paper.

"We shoulda painted the whole room," Deena muttered below me, where she was helping. "We'd be done by now, and I could be shopping with Karla instead of doing *this*."

Anger flared inside me. "No way! Why should *I* have to do everything? Besides, this looks better. And it's faster."

"It is not." Deena gave the wet paper a yank. It was her job to put the bottom half in place and then hand me the next section to put up.

"Careful!" I snapped. "It tears easy, remember?"

"The stupid thing's crooked."

"It shouldn't be. You must've put it up crooked."

"I did not. You did the top, so it's your fault. Besides, the stupid wall's crooked. How'm I supposed to make it look right if the walls aren't straight?"

I looked down and saw that Deena was right. Even though the seams fit together near the ceiling where I'd been working, there were whitish gaps near the floor. "How come you didn't tell me sooner?" I yelled. "Now we can't change it. You've wasted so much paper already there won't be enough to fix it."

Anger burned in my sister's brown eyes. "You always blame everything on me. It's not *my* fault Mom decided to move."

"You — " But I broke off. Deena was in one of her impossible moods. There was no way I'd be able to reason with her. I drew in a long breath. My head was pounding. "Let's loosen this strip. Maybe we can fix it — it's still wet." Keeping my feet steady on the ladder, I carefully eased the paper away from the wall. Beneath me it moved in a convulsive jerk.

"Aaack!" Deena yelped. "It ripped!"

"How can you be so dumb?" I wailed. "Now we'll never have enough. If we have to buy more, *you* can pay for it. Have you got ten extra bucks?"

"Girls!" Mom's shocked voice startled us into silence. The long strip of wet wallpaper slipped out of my hands and draped over Deena. I sputtered with convulsive giggles, then looked around. Mom was standing in the doorway. How long had she been there? She was supposed to be at work.

The paper writhed and Deena's furious face appeared. "Now look what you did. I bet you did it on purpose. I quit!"

My mouth opened, but Mom spoke first. "Honestly, you two — you're going at one another like a couple of fighting dogs. Is *this* how you behave when I'm at work?"

Mom looked awful. Her face was the colour of oatmeal, all except for black hollows beneath her eyes.

"Mom . . ." I said hesitantly, "are you all right?"

"I have one of my headaches. The *last* thing I need is to come home and find the two of you acting like this . . ." She went on and on.

"Sorry," Deena mumbled when Mom started winding down.

"Yeah." I sat on a box and glared at the stained carpet. "It's just *so hard*." The words popped out, almost by themselves. "There's too much to do, and I don't really know how to do it, and Deena — " I bit down. This wasn't the kind of thing Mom needed to hear. But I couldn't stop. Deep inside, something was prodding me on. It wasn't right to expect a sixteen-year-old to do practically all the packing and moving, especially with no car. *And* keep her bratty sister in line. "Deena doesn't do her share. How — "

"I do so!" Deena's voice went shrill. She stomped her foot. The floor squeaked.

I stood up. "You do not! I have to do all the work and it's not fair! Everybody thinks I'm a slave. 'Sammie, do this. Sammie, do that. Sammie, don't forget . . .' I can't even take time off to go to the *bathroom* without being told to do something."

Mom's face flushed. Suddenly her eyes were glittering. "How do you think *I* feel?" Her voice whipped out at me. "On my feet twelve hours a day, working myself to death for two selfish girls who take it all for granted. It's not *my* fault your father refused to buy insurance; Lord knows I tried to convince him, but no, he was so sure he'd be around till he was a hundred and four. It's not *my* fault he got sick. Is this the kind of thanks I get? When I try to provide you girls with a home?"

I stared in disbelief. This wasn't Mom. It was Aunt Vivian in disguise. Only a million times worse. My own headache exploded into a pounding desperation that churned through me. My feet stamped across the squeaky, slanted floor. They pushed me out the door, but stopped long enough to let me slam it with all my strength. The bang reverberated off the neighbouring houses. A grey shingle skittered off the roof and fell onto the gravel where there should have been a lawn. Or a flower bed. And then my feet pounded along unfamiliar sidewalks while tears streamed down my face.

How could she? It wasn't — how could she — wasn't fair — nobody appreciated me — why should I have to put up with all that — *How could she?* Why'd I have to get stuck with such a rotten life, and be expected to do everything for everybody else in the world, and nobody gave a damn about my feelings or what was fair or — *How could she?*

My feet found air where they expected pavement. I sprawled forward into the street. There was a squeal of brakes. I shrank, expecting crushing pain. None, only the burn of scraped flesh. I rocked to my feet and was applauded. Shrill whistles sounded. It was a carload of sailors. "Hey, want a beer?" one yelled. They all laughed, a loud burst of male power.

A new panic set my feet in motion. The car crept along beside me. They called out all kinds of things Blake might say. Wildly I looked around but didn't have the faintest idea where I was. How could I have been so stupid?

I rounded a corner and saw a small Chinese grocery store. Winded, I ran inside and pretended to look for something. My cramps were a gnawing ache. I lingered by the boxes of cereal, hoping nobody would notice me. But that wasn't likely. There were no customers. I looked at detergents in bright containers. Some of the bottles on the back of the shelf were dusty.

The sensible thing would be to find my way home. But why should I? It wasn't fair, the way Mom was treating me. Besides, what if the sailors came back? I walked down a crammed aisle, past the notepads and pens. The plastic wrap on the packages of envelopes looked ancient.

"Can I help you?" An equally ancient voice sounded from the back of the store.

I wondered if I should just leave. Instead, I went to find the woman, passing curiously fragrant parcels all labeled in Chinese. "I — I'm new in this part of town and got lost. Can I use your phone?"

"You don't want to buy something?" The old woman had white hair and piercing dark eyes that challenged me to say no.

"I — " I gulped in some air. "I'm sorry, I don't have my purse. Some sailors were following me and I got scared, and — "

She stared at me a moment longer and then wordlessly pulled an old black telephone out from under the counter. She slapped it down with surprising force, then shuffled over to sit on a high stool, all the while watching me.

My fingers trembled as I dialed. "Hi, Glenna? Can you come get me? I'm lost. Some sailors were following me, and I got scared, and — "

"Sammie! Where are you?" My half-sister's concerned voice made me go limp with relief.

"I don't know exactly. The Star Confectionery, I think."

"Just a sec. I'll check the phone book." Through the receiver I could hear pages riffling, and Willie crying, "Mam! Mam!"

"Found it," Glenna said a moment later. "But I can't pick you up. Greg's got the car." She hesitated. "Something else wrong, Sammie?"

I wanted to babble it all out but couldn't with the old woman glaring at me. "Yeah," I mumbled. "Mom and I had a fight, and I feel so — "

"Come on over," Glenna said. "It's only ten or twelve blocks. And don't worry about those sailors. They're probably just bored and looking for a little excitement. I doubt if they'll wait around — usually they just keep on cruising. If they *are* still there, call me right back. I'll pop Willie in the stroller, and we'll come meet you."

I blinked fast as I listened to Glenna's instructions. Then I thanked the old woman and promised to buy something next time.

When I walked into Glenna's apartment I could smell food cooking. Real food, not something out of a can. Colourful posters made the walls look alive, and there were no boxes stacked anywhere.

"Hi, kiddo." Glenna looked knowingly at me as Willie clung to her legs. "So life's tough, eh?"

I burst into tears all over again.

"Come on, have a seat, but don't flood my couch." Glenna steered me over to sit down. "Fifty bucks an hour, so make sure you get it all out."

I managed a weak laugh. "I haven't even got my purse. Can I charge it?" As I told her about Mom and all the problems, Willie started bringing me things — books, stuffed toys, advertising flyers. After a while my lap was full. And then Willie decided to climb up to show me everything all over again.

Glenna chuckled. "Get down, Willie. Sammie doesn't have any space left in her lap." She grinned at me. "Once you sit down, you're a sitting duck. And since I'm old news, you get all the attention."

"It's okay," I mumbled. The feel of Willie's little self cuddled against me, shoving each item in front of my nose for inspection, was oddly comforting. He was so untouched by the chaos at our place. And that somehow made it better.

"This business with your mom." Glenna's voice went serious. "I think what she really needs is a man around to help out."

"Oh sure!" I burst out. "Get Mom a boyfriend and everything's solved. Anyway, Uncle Amos has been — "

"That's not what I mean." Glenna brushed her dark hair away from her forehead. "It's the whole role thing. Here she is, working two jobs, which she can't handle, plus taking care of you and Deena, plus moving . . ."

Willie thrust a red ball in my face. "Bah!" he cried.

I took the ball and rolled it across the carpet. "Go get the ball, Willie." He slid down.

I drew in a deep breath. "And that leaves *me* taking care of me and Deena and the house, plus the moving, and *I* can't handle that, either. Plus school. Why can't Deena — "

"Of course you can't handle it," Glenna interrupted. "It's too much. And Deena's just a kid, so you can't really expect — "

My foot came down with a thud. "It's not fair."

"Life's never fair, kiddo. I don't want to sound critical, but it maybe wasn't the greatest, selling the car before you guys moved. Greg and I'll help all we can, but I really don't see a way around it without — " She broke off and giggled. "Not unless you can convince your mom to get herself a wife. Now *that* might be the answer — "

"Bah!" Willie was back, ball in one hand and an apple core in the other.

"That's gross, Willie," Glenna said. "We don't take things out of the garbage."

Willie put the apple core in his mouth.

"No." Glenna scooped him up and disappeared into the kitchen. I heard a loud wail. When they returned Glenna was carrying Willie and a plastic bowl full of Cheerios.

I resented Glenna's suggestion that we needed a man to make everything work out. At the same time, I couldn't help remembering how it had been with Dad around, at our old house. Mom had been so different. Relaxed. Softer. She'd worked part-time at a neighbourhood day care, and she used to laugh a lot. Play the piano. She always planted a big garden. And she was always reading, sometimes sewing neat things. Talk about the easy life. Maybe *she* was the one who missed it most of all.

I sat there watching Willie play with his Cheerios. "What's the matter with *woman*power?" I muttered. "Women can do the same stuff as men."

Glenna smiled. "Sure they can. The problem is, kiddo, women still don't get paid half as much, so they have to work twice as hard for the same money."

I thought of our old house — how Mom's full-time job at the drugstore couldn't cover living expenses plus the mortgage. We'd been numb when we moved out. Numb because of Dad's cancer, what it was doing to him, to all of us. Now the numbness was gone. What was the matter with me? It was almost March. Over a year since Dad died, and still . . .

"You haven't had a heavy-duty boyfriend yet," Glenna went on. "A person like that gets to be such a major part of your life that they almost seem like part of you. You work things out so that what needs doing gets done. Your mom had what — seventeen, eighteen? — years of that. And now . . ."

I picked at the ratty upholstery on Glenna's old couch. "I'm sick of hearing about Mom."

Glenna patted my arm. "I know how you feel. But I think the kid and I'll walk over to let her know you're okay."

I stiffened.

"Relax, kiddo. You need a break. Once everything quiets down, let's you and me hop on a ferry and get some fresh air. Hey, maybe we could even go down to Seattle for a weekend, get a motel room, shop . . . Just you and me, okay? Willie could visit his grandma part of the time . . ."

I gave her a weak smile. It would be a lot of fun to do that with Glenna. But the way I was feeling, I didn't want her to have the satisfaction of knowing.

She grabbed the *TV Guide* and bopped me on the head. "You're so thrilled I can't get over it. Make yourself at home. Go scream in the shower, if that's what turns you on. Drink the Coke in the fridge. But whatever you do, *don't* eat the last cookie in the tin. I'm saving it for my own private snack when Greg goes over his claims files this evening."

I sat there watching as Glenna dressed Willie in his jacket and toque. "Have fun," I said half-heartedly as they went out. Glenna stuck out her tongue at me.

The silence was stunning. For a moment I wished I'd brought my homework so I could get some of it done. But who cared about homework? I wandered around the place. Nothing needed doing. I flipped through some of Glenna's magazines. The fashions and makeup articles rubbed me the wrong way. I got up and found CBC-FM on the stereo, poured myself some Coke, and ran a bath, using some of Glenna's bath oil.

It was heaven soaking, with the water silky-warm around me. As my shoulders and neck began relaxing, my headache eased. How long had it been there? All I could remember was feeling like this, pinched and tight, for weeks. I submerged and let the heat of the water touch my face, my scalp. Wonderful. I blew bubbles, feeling the air tickle my nostrils. When I came up to breathe I felt much better.

Something familiar was playing on the radio. I sat up, listening. The Beethoven violin concerto. The tones touched something inside me, catching me off guard. Memories of the time at the hospital with Blake's violin flooded through me. Matt's pain was so raw and fresh, compared to mine. I wondered what he was doing now. Then I thought of Mom, so tired she looked half-dead, and I nearly cried. The violin kept singing in a comforting kind of way.

By the time the piece was over the water had cooled. I wrapped up in a giant towel and studied myself in the mirror. Glenna's talk about boyfriends was disturbing. Would anybody ever feel that way about me? And would it be somebody I wanted? Deena spent half her time moping over one guy or another. She could open the Sears catalogue and swoon over the male models every time. To me they just looked like a bunch of dorks standing there in their underwear, or pyjamas.

"Don't worry, Sammie," Mom had told me once, about three years ago — when she still had time to talk to us, before Dad got really sick. "It takes time to find the right person. Don't rush. It's more important to find yourself first."

The phone began ringing. I let it ring, but it kept on shrilling, like Aunt Vivian's nagging. "Oh shut up," I said. It didn't. So I answered it.

"Sammie. Where the hell were you?" It was Glenna, and her voice was sharp.

"In the tub," I hedged.

"Get over here as fast as you can. Your mom — "

"I'm all wet. My hair — " And then Glenna's words sank in. "What happened?" I croaked. "Where are you, anyhow?"

"At the neighbour's. Mrs. — " She broke off. I heard voices in the background. "Mrs. Crosbie's. She says you've already met."

I clutched the receiver in both hands. *"What's wrong with Mom?"* I screamed.

"Maybe nothing serious. She thinks it's palpitations." But Glenna sounded incredibly nervous.

No! A kind of paralysis clamped over me. *Not Mom too!*

"Sammie?" Glenna's voice. "You still there? Hey, don't fall apart, kiddo. She'll be all right, don't worry. Turn the oven off, will you? And grab the diaper bag for me on your way out."

Seventeen

My run back to the house on Helm Street was very different from my tumultuous exit. It was beginning to get dark. The adrenaline was pumping so hard I was scarcely aware of my surroundings, only my wet hair flapping in my face and Willie's diaper bag knocking around my knees. And Mom.

There were no words for the panic and guilt that battered at me. Except, maybe, like being in a kayak on the open sea, with gale-force winds blowing.

I leaned on the doorbell at Mrs. Crosbie's house and could hardly make myself wait for someone to answer. Finally Deena did. Mom lay on the couch with a brown plaid blanket over her. Her face was ashen. "Mom . . ." I gulped. I wanted to run to her but was afraid it might make her worse.

She turned toward me. "Sammie . . ." She held out her arms.

I went to her. "Mom, I'm so sorry — "

"Oh Sammie, *I'm* the one who's sorry. I had no right — " Mom broke off in tears and pulled me against her. "You mean the world to me, love. What I said was unforgivable."

"Don't worry, Mom, it's okay." I could hear her heart thudding like a metronome set on *presto*. But it lacked the steady beat, racing along for a while, pausing for a terrifying moment, only to resume its erratic pace all over again. I bit down hard, praying nonstop to a God I wasn't sure was listening.

"Don't get worked up, dear." Mrs. Crosbie's concerned voice cut in. "You need to rest."

"I still say we should call an ambulance." Glenna was somewhere across the room.

"No," Mom said into my hair. "Call Amos and Vivian."

I shuddered. "A taxi would be faster."

"Not at rush hour," Glenna countered.

"I'll go get Mr. O'Reilly across the street," Mrs. Crosbie announced. "I'm sure he'll be willing." She was gone before any of us could argue.

"This is hardly the way I'd hoped to meet the neighbours," Mom said tartly.

Mr. O'Reilly was huge and balding. "Sure, I'll take you in," he said. "Shall I, er, carry you?"

Mom's face flickered. "I can walk, thanks." Very slowly she sat up. "Sammie, if you'd just — "

I helped her up. "Can somebody get my purse? Mom's too. And the house key."

Silently Deena held them up for me to see. Her face was frightened.

Even leaning on my arm, Mom moved with halting steps.

"Here, I'll push the young fella in the stroller." Mrs. Crosbie's voice. Glenna came around to take Mom's other arm.

"Which hospital?" Mr. O'Reilly called as he headed across the street to start his car.

"The General," Mom said faintly.

How many times had she taken Dad there? I'd lost track. There'd been so many trips. The last time had been that terrifying morning when he fell down the stairs because he was going paralyzed. My eyes burned. Now Mom. "Don't worry, Mom," I said. "We're with you. And you'll be fine." I hoped I was right.

"Deena can stay with me," Glenna offered. "They won't want Willie running around Emergency."

"But — " Deena and I both protested. I'd been counting on having Glenna there to know what to do.

"That would be fine." Mom sounded weaker. She leaned more heavily on my arm. "Or call Vivian; she won't mind."

"But I want to go too," Deena whined.

I glared at my sister as Mr. O'Reilly parked his station wagon, then opened the door for Mom. I helped her into the front seat and scooted in behind. Deena handed me the purses and stood there. Her chin was trembling.

Glenna put her arm around Deena. "Call as soon as you know anything," she said.

I nodded but didn't have time to answer.

Going to Emergency intensified the nightmare. Mr. O'Reilly dropping us off. The cold fluorescent light. Registering Mom, seeing her wheeled away. Wondering . . . The wait took forever. Parents brought in crying children. An accident victim was carried in on a stretcher, already connected to an IV. The ambulance attendants moved with quick efficiency. Explosive bursts of static on their radios sounded like gunfire I'd heard on the news. And the lights overhead flickered in a way that made me incredibly hyper.

At last a nurse came for me. "Is she all right?" I asked hoarsely.

The nurse smiled. "I don't think it's anything serious. Dr. Singh has just seen her, and we've put in a call to your family doctor."

I went faint with relief.

Mom lay on a narrow examining table wearing a partly fastened blue hospital gown. Electrodes were attached to her chest with weird round stickers, and she was hooked up to a monitor. The pattern of her heartbeat darted across the screen in glowing green traces. Flashing numbers showed her heart rate.

"Mom — " I said. "You're all right?"

She gave me a wan smile. "It was palpitations, like I thought. They've stopped. But my blood pressure's way up and they may keep me overnight for observation."

I sank into a chair. "The nurse said they called Dr. Karopoulos?"

Mom nodded. "You wouldn't happen to have your gloves, would you? My fingers are ice cubes."

I fumbled in my pockets. "No gloves," I said. I reached for one of Mom's frigid hands and held it tightly.

"Thanks," she said with a shaky laugh. "I got so scared, thinking what might happen to you girls if something was really wrong."

I drew in a sharp breath. "You're going to be fine, Mom."

She nodded again. "I know. But in case anything *does* ever happen, I have insurance. If I get stuck in here and can't work for a while, well, there's insurance for that too. After all we've been through, I'm not taking any chances."

"Don't talk like that!" I begged.

"Topic closed. I just needed to let you know."

We waited in silence. It was hard to sit still. "I should phone Glenna and tell her you're okay," I said.

"That would be a good idea." Mom squeezed my hand.

I made the call, but couldn't settle down. My stomach was growly. The clocks said it was already seven-thirty. I dawdled on my way back to Mom's cubicle in Emergency. She was going to be all right. I just couldn't face any more green numbers. Or gleaming instruments sitting ready on shelves, or packages of sterile dressings. I went to the vending machines and bought a hot chocolate, then looked through the windows of the gift shop, where I'd browsed so many hours during Dad's long illness.

When I returned, Dr. Karopoulos was in the room with Mom.

"Your mother's going to be fine," he told me on his way out. "I'm going to keep her here for a few days. She's badly rundown, and we need to get her blood pressure back to normal."

Dazed, I nodded. We'd manage. Just knowing that Mom would be all right was the main thing.

She gave me a rueful smile. "I'm sorry, Sammie. This is the worst possible time for — "

Dr. Karopoulos spun around. "Don't apologize, Carolyn. You've been through several years of major stress and haven't allowed yourself to recover. Now your body's decided to make you do it. That's why I'm keeping you here, so you won't go right back and keep overworking."

Mom sighed. "I know, it all makes perfect sense. It's just that we're supposed to be moving next week."

Dr. Karopoulos snorted. "Moving? That's major stress. I'm tempted to keep you here even longer, in that case."

"Don't worry, Mom," I said. "We'll manage. You just get better."

A few minutes later a porter arrived to take Mom up to the ward. I tagged along to help her get settled, promising to call Uncle Amos.

Their line was busy. And Glenna said Greg was still at the office, so she couldn't come get me. I checked both Mom's and my wallets. There wasn't enough cash for taxi fare, and I felt uneasy about using my bus pass at night, alone, whether I went back to Glenna's place or to the apartment. I called Jen, but her sister Lisa said Jen had gone somewhere. Their parents were out with the other car, so there was no chance of getting a ride with the Cascardis.

A horrible caged feeling pressed in on me. The intercom announced the end of visiting hours. I tried Aunt Vivian again with my last quarter, but the line was still busy. The quarter clattered down in the coin return. My hand slipped into my purse and found the square corners of a card. I pulled it out and looked at Julie's number.

I hesitated, then called.

Julie walked into the main lobby half an hour later. "How is she?" she asked.

I still felt dazed and exhausted. "She's going to be okay."

Julie's gleaming hair bounced against her shoulders. "Good. It must've been scary. You've already had your share of bad news." As she swung around, she looked at the clock. "You wouldn't want to go say hi to Matt, would you?"

The thought had never crossed my mind. "I'm tired. Besides, it's late. I doubt they'll let us on the ward."

"We could always try." When I didn't answer, Julie sauntered over to the information desk. She looked oddly unsettled as she returned. "He's been discharged!"

A new wave of relief rushed through me. Matt was in rehab, at last. Suddenly I was so tired I had to sit down. The whole day had been too much.

Julie looked closely at me. "Are you okay? You look really fried."

"No. I mean, yes. I mean — I can't even think." I sank back in the soft chair. "I'll just go to sleep for a couple of hours."

"They'd stick you with loitering."

I was so exhausted I giggled. "You mean your dad doesn't own the hospital too?"

"Not funny." Julie sounded disgusted. "Up, woman. I'm here to take you home. Or somewhere."

The cool air helped pull my head back together. "It's been bad lately," I muttered. "Absolutely insane."

"I know the feeling." Julie led the way to her car. "Actually, I can't complain," she said as she unlocked. "My deah mothah is in Paris for five lovely months. And Daddy's in Geneva, then off to a series of meetings in New York."

"Then who — " I bit off the rest of my question. It wasn't my business.

"Maisie and I get along just fine." Julie glanced at me as she slid behind the wheel. "Our housekeeper. Actually, she's quite human. When I was little I used to pretend she was my real mother, only she was so poor she couldn't afford to keep me, so my parents bought me and then gave her a job so she could stay with me. But — " Julie sighed " — I have my father's nose and my mother's wrists and earlobes; and my blood type is what you'd logically get by combining theirs. So I guess my parentage is not in doubt. Too bad."

"Could we stop at The Junction?" I blurted out. "I haven't eaten."

"No prob." Julie flicked the turn signal and veered into the centre lane. All around us headlights and taillights danced like moving beacons. Only we weren't on the water, we were in the middle of Qualicum Drive. No, maybe it was Sutherland, it was hard to tell because I was so tired . . .

"Sammie. I said, are you still breathing?"

Julie's voice cut into my foggy awareness. I jumped. "Huh? I — What did you say? Are we there?"

She laughed. "I said, I have an idea. We had an ultra-scrumpy roast for dinner, and there was lots left. Why don't you come home with me and let Maisie fix you a snack?"

"Uh . . ." I was too tired to think. "Okay. I'll call Glenna so she won't worry."

"Excellent." Julie hit the turn signal and we turned off the main thoroughfare, following a Scenic Drive sign. We continued along the road for a while, into neighbourhoods that became more and more exclusive. Floodlights illumined well-manicured gardens and huge homes set back from the road. "That's where His Holiness Harris-Hughes lives," Julie said abruptly. Her voice was derisive as she jabbed her left elbow toward one such house. "I'm going to challenge that cold-blooded salamander. He's an absolute amphibian — figures he's done pretty well for himself by crawling out of the swamp and into principal violin. But let me tell you, he reeks of the bog."

"Hope you win." I couldn't pull my mind away from Mom. Julie's talk seemed like empty words. In a way I wished I'd taken the bus. I leaned against the headrest and closed my eyes as the car swayed around curves in the road, climbing slightly. At last it stopped.

Dogs barked. I opened my eyes to yet another floodlit house set back among trees.

"We're here," Julie said tersely.

I got out. Except for the barking dogs, stillness surrounded us. Off to one direction, through gaps in the foliage, city lights lay in geometric patterns far below. In another was blackness that had to be the strait, for beyond it were a few faint twinkles, while still another light was slowly crossing the darkness. Overhead were stars, more than I ever saw at home.

The house looked like something you'd see in a magazine. I felt like an intruder in my old jeans and sweatshirt, as though I'd get the place dirty just by looking at it, maybe even get arrested. But Julie didn't seem to notice, moving with uncaring strides through the opulence. "Maisie?" she called. "I've brought Sammie, and she hasn't eaten. Would you mind fixing her something?"

My face went hot. It had been wrong to come. If I'd taken the bus, Glenna would've fed me whatever it was I'd smelled cooking, and then Deena and I would've slept in the living room. Or gone to Aunt Vivian's.

"Oh, the poor dear!" A decidedly Scottish voice came from somewhere. I followed Julie toward it and then relaxed. Maisie Ross was nothing like the house. Stout and frumpy, she sat me down in the huge kitchen and fussed over me while Julie stood there filling her in on things I hadn't realized she'd known about me. I was fed, with Mozart playing softly in the background, then offered a soak in the Jacuzzi. Droopy tired in a borrowed bathing suit, my hair stringy wet, I wandered back into the kitchen later with Julie, only to be invited to sleep over. Glenna gave permission without even asking when I'd be back.

Tired as I was, it was hard to get to sleep. The borrowed nightgown felt silky and strange compared to my comfy flannels. The bed was huge and foreign. Julie said the room was actually her practice room, but that it had to double as guest room. She was down the hall, for it seemed there were no rooms with two beds.

Images of Mom rushed at me. Her shouting. The frightening grey tone of her face as she lay on Mrs. Crosbie's couch, the frantic racing of her heart. The hospital scenes replayed themselves, sometimes with Dad sneaking in too. I got up and went to the French doors, parted the luxuriant draperies, but there was no view of downtown, only tree silhouettes and the black gap of water. I wished Deena were with me, with her snoring and sleep-talking — anything to reassure me that Mom really would be all right. That life could still be normal. That what had happened was in no way my fault.

I dreamed. We were together, Dad, Mom, Deena, me. We were leaving for a picnic on Waite Island. A gale was blowing and I knew the flat open ferry would be tossed like a cast-off paper plate on the heaving sea. But we hadn't gone out the door yet. Dad's face changed, got skinnier, until a fleshless skull grinned at us. "Bill," Mom said, "I think we'd better not go. It's too stormy." Couldn't she see that it wasn't Dad anymore? I tried to warn her, but my voice didn't work. "It's time to go," the skeleton-Dad insisted, and as I watched, the numbers fell off the clock, leaving a terrifying blank face, and Mom shrank into an old woman in a blue hospital gown with electrodes attached to her chest. "Deena!" I cried. "Stop him!" But Deena had turned into Willie, and was sitting on the floor holding her bottle upside down. "It's time to go, Carolyn." Dad took Mom by the hand. "No!" I wailed. "We need Mom!" I grabbed for her, but the grinning skeleton pulled her into the air and they vanished. All I got was a fleeting touch of hospital gown. "No!" I screamed. "No! I hate you!" I cried and cried, but nobody was there to hear.

Everything was shaking. Earthquake! I tried to yell out but my voice didn't work anymore. The shaking continued until it felt like my teeth would rattle right out.

"Sammie!" I opened my eyes and saw Julie's face. Her hands were on my shoulders. "You were screaming," she said.

I sat up. The dream lingered like a foul odour.

My face was wet with tears, and as I gulped in a breath, I started shuddering.

Julie sat down beside me. "Are you all right? You scared me."

"I dreamed my mom — " It sounded stupid, blurting out a nightmare like a little kid, and I quit. But I was so frightened I had to gasp for breath. "I'm afraid something — " I couldn't finish.

In a matter-of-fact way Julie pulled the telephone off the bedside table. She dialed, waited. The clock radio said 3:17. "I'm calling about Mrs. Franklin; she was admitted several hours ago with palpitations and high blood pressure." Pause. "Her daughter." Another pause, a long one. Julie repeated the information casually as if it were mid-afternoon, not three in the morning. Another short pause. "Thanks so much." She hung up and turned to me. "'Mrs. Franklin is sleeping quietly; her blood pressure has dropped a bit.'"

I wiped my eyes. "Thanks. You're incredible. I mean, pulling it off like it was any old time of day . . ."

"I had some practice calling about Matt." Julie got up quickly, opened the drapes. Moonlight silvered the water, and silhouettes of Douglas fir reached upward with a calm strength. "Want anything? Since we're both awake."

I was still trembly. "Hot chocolate, maybe? If it's not too much trouble."

"Trouble?" Julie gave a laugh I couldn't interpret. "No trouble, miss. Wait here and I shall provide."

A fleeting uneasiness darted through me, but something else argued back. Julie acted like someone who didn't have much practice at being friends. Several minutes later she returned, carrying a tray. China cups and saucers clattered momentarily as she set the tray down.

"And now some music." Julie crossed the room, pushed buttons on a wall stereo, slid a compact disc into the player. Sombre notes, deep and slow, filled the room. "Mahler," she announced. She took a cup and saucer from the tray, then sat on the lushly carpeted floor and gazed out over the water.

After a few minutes I joined her on the carpet. My shivering eased with the warmth of the drink. Outside, the moon played hide-and-seek like poetry in the light clouds. The music went on and on, forever unfolding, touching me deep inside with a mystical power. It was like seeing the universe, like all-knowing intuition. Calmness seeped into me. It had been a scary dream, that was all. Mom was going to be all right.

Yet as I glanced sideways at Julie, I noticed a deep sadness lingering in her face.

Eighteen

Mom was in the hospital for nine days. Dr. Karopoulos insisted he needed to monitor her blood pressure closely so he could decide whether or not to put her on medication. Mom said it was just a power play to keep her from going back to work, since her blood pressure had been almost normal after the fourth day. At any rate, she was in long enough for the insurance to start paying. More important, Mom began looking like herself again. Her face regained its colour, while the dark hollows beneath her eyes gradually faded. She looked so much more rested that, in a way, I didn't mind her long absence.

We moved on schedule, two days before Mom came home. It was a crazy time with Aunt Vivian and Uncle Amos, and Glenna and Greg all bustling around, each trying to do things their own way. Deena and I kept cracking up over how the grown-ups bossed each other around. Mrs. Crosbie was in and out, bringing cups of tea, sandwiches and, once, plates of cake and ice cream. Blake never showed up. Thank goodness. And Deena and I were getting along perfectly for a change — why not, with four adults all trying to take full responsibility? It was great to get a break.

But they wouldn't let us stay at our new house alone. Aunt Vivian moved in until Mom was discharged. It was a long two days, but at least I didn't have to cook.

And then there was the piano. I didn't have the faintest clue until the last minute. Aunt V seemed to be a genius at keeping us busy that morning. She told Deena to go buy some flowers. That meant a walk of seven or eight blocks to the little Chinese grocery store where I'd called Glenna that awful day. Deena complained because it was raining, but eventually she went. Aunt Vivian told me to pick out some fresh clothes for Mom to wear coming home, and I could've kicked myself for not thinking of that myself. So I spent a long time looking through Mom's closet, trying to figure out what she'd like.

When I heard men's voices and loud thumping, scraping sounds, I wondered what we'd forgotten to move. The apartment had been bare when we left, an empty cell with no imprint of our lives. I went to see what was going on.

There it was, an old upright piano on a dolly. Uncle Amos and Greg and two other men wrestled with it, panting, while Aunt Vivian stood in the centre of our living room giving orders.

"A piano?" I gasped.

Aunt Vivian turned to me and smiled. "Your uncle found it at an estate sale," she said. "We thought your mother would enjoy a house-warming gift."

"Oh Aunt Vivian! Thanks!" I threw my arms around her, though it was rather like hugging a parking meter.

She acted surprised, brushing her hair back from her face, but she patted my shoulder. "Carolyn has had some hard times. With a new start, let's hope she can put it all behind her."

Dad too? It stung, but I kept quiet. As Mom so often said, Aunt Vivian meant well; she just wasn't very tactful.

Deena walked in, drenched, with a handful of daffodils and tulips wrapped in newspaper. "A piano!" she yelped. "Where'd it come from?" Without waiting for a reply, she dropped the flowers on the coffee table and went over to strike a few notes.

"Stay out of their way, Deena." Once again my aunt's voice was cross.

Uncle Amos brought Mom home an hour later. She gave a little cry when she saw the piano. "Oh, you shouldn't have," she protested. In the confusion of hugs and pats on the shoulder, I saw her wipe tears from her eyes several times.

Of course she asked Aunt Vivian and Uncle Amos to stay for tea. But it worked out all right. Rain drummed on the roof as we all sat there in the living room. It streaked down the windows, but the whispering oil furnace kept the dampness out, and the flowers were like a patch of sunlight on the china cabinet. I slumped on the footstool feeling incredibly relaxed and cozy. Mom met my eyes with such a warm, loving look that I knew for sure she'd truly come home.

Our old house sold soon afterwards. Mom quit her waitressing job and spent her spare time puttering around the place in jeans and her old university sweatshirt. She painted the windowsills and door frames, read, even dug a garden plot. And of course she spent hours at the piano.

Deena surprised us and got a job delivering flyers. She brought home a grey tabby kitten one day and named him Dominic after the lead guitar player in Smooth Dudes. She even paid for his shots. And new friends from her new school gradually began dropping by and tying up the phone.

Jen and Tomás Díaz became inseparable that spring. A lonely emptiness hounded me at school as I watched the two of them in the corridors and at lunch, but I couldn't bring myself to wish they'd break up just so I'd have my best friend back. Jen was really happy, glowing with a sudden radiant beauty. I couldn't wish *that* away.

After school it wasn't as bad. Roger, Mom's boss, gave me a job at the pharmacy two afternoons a week plus Saturdays. I worked in the stock room, unpacking boxes of pills and over-the-counter goods, checking invoices, and putting on price tags. Actually, it was kind of fun. Sometimes I stood there talking to Todd, the delivery boy, when he was between runs. On my days off I practised a lot and took walks around the neighbourhood. It left me with a funny feeling, knowing that Dad might have gone along the same sidewalks, years and years ago as a kid. Mixed in with all that was a kind of melancholy, as if I'd failed Matt, abandoning him right when things were getting better. For some reason I couldn't bring myself to visit him at the rehab hospital.

Julie came over occasionally, but she was often busy studying or practising long hours so she could challenge Geoff Harris-Hughes for principal violin. She won. With her as concert master the whole violin section came alive. Geoff looked sulky and put-out for a while. Julie gloated. And the Beethoven violin concerto reappeared in our music folders one day following our performance at the all-province music festival in early April.

Excited, I caught Julie after rehearsal. "Are you playing the solo part?" I asked.

She smiled sardonically. "I trust not. I'm stand-in."

For an instant a stillness came around me in the noisy rehearsal room. "You mean . . . ?"

Julie nodded. Her eyes went soft. Then Julie Blaustein actually blushed, in the midst of forty-two kids packing away their instruments.

* * *

The night I'd stayed over at Julie's, the night of Mom's palpitations, Julie said something that stuck with me. "Friends. Everybody says they help you sort things out. I wouldn't know." She'd hesitated, with a cautious glance at me. "With Matt I could *talk*, until . . ." She bent to inspect her toenails. "But I expect it's different, anyhow, with a guy. With you I can tell there's lots beneath the surface." Again, the cautious, quizzical glance. "When I need to work things out I turn on my Mahler. And talk to my tape recorder. It never tells me to shut up."

I needed a friend that spring of so many changes. Although Julie seemed to need one too, she was hard to get close to. Sometimes she was there, but often not. And so I found it hard to open up about what hadn't changed. Needing to get a sense of Dad, who he'd been, and how all that fit with who I was.

And the nightmares. The one at Julie's house seemed to open a channel for many more. Several nights a week I'd wake up screaming. Dad coming back for Mom. Dad alone on the beach with a tsunami rolling in, enormous, glassy-green, terrifying. Dad grinning from his wheelchair, grasping the outer metal rims and rolling fast, faster, faster, toward a flight of hundreds of stairs. The skeleton Dad grabbing me. Fighting back, forcing the skull face away with the flat of my hand, pushing, twisting, until first the teeth would fall out, and suddenly it would disintegrate with a clatter into a heap of bones at my feet. Those nights I'd wake up bathed in a cold sweat. And then I'd cry.

It got so I was afraid to go to sleep.

Some nights Deena would glower at me and threaten to sleep on the couch. But she never did. Within a few minutes she'd always be snoring softly. While I'd lie there. Afraid of the scary blank space between waking and sleeping. Afraid that if I let go, I might never come back.

Mom fixed me lots of hot chocolate in our kitchen with the slanting floors. We'd sit there at three in the morning, she drowsy, sipping the warm fluid that made the world sane again. Sometimes she'd play a tape, sometimes folk groups from the sixties, sometimes Brahms piano music. Sometimes I told her about the dreams, but after a while it got repetitious. One night she pulled out a box of old photos. I sorted through them, longingly looking at ones of Dad, as tears wet my face.

Mom phoned all over about counselling. We couldn't really afford it. She tried the youth clinic, but was told they dealt with drug and alcohol crises. Incest. Rape. Suicide attempts. Nightmares about a dead father didn't rate.

I tried Julie's idea of talking to a blank tape during odd moments when I was the only one home. But I felt like a total nerd. Even Dominic would look at me strangely and meow to be let out, or come and rub against my face until I had to laugh. So I started writing everything down in a notebook that I kept hidden under the piano.

* * *

In the midst of all of that I saw Matt again, completely by accident.

It was Saturday morning and I was at work. Mom said the week had been hectic; a lot of the shelves needed re-stocking and I seemed to be making dozens of trips between the dispensary and the stock room, which was in the basement. I'd finished putting disposable diapers on the shelves, and I was sitting on the floor unpacking tubes of ointment for diaper rash when a cool draft from the door caught my bare arms. I only looked up because the door was open an awfully long time.

While someone stood outside holding the heavy glass door, a tall guy in a wheelchair was struggling to get across the threshold. His head was bent with the effort, so I couldn't see his face. But the sight of reddish-brown hair and a Walkman headset sent shock waves jangling through me. His leg cast was gone.

As I watched, the person outside said something to Matt. He shook his head and went into a spasm of coughing. Then he looked up and saw me. I rocked to my feet and went to him, while Mom watched from the cash register. I grasped the armrest on his chair, giving a firm tug, which pulled the wheels across the threshold. "Sometimes people have trouble with that," I said. I neglected to add that it was usually elderly people or mothers with strollers.

Matt just shook his head. He had the bleary look of someone with a terrible cold. "Thanks," he muttered. A dull flush crept into his cheeks. He fumbled in his jacket pocket for something, a prescription, and wheeled over to my mom at the cash register.

My own face went hot. Feeling slapped, I turned back to the diaper rash ointments.

"It's Sammie, isn't it?"

I looked up in surprise. Matt's mother was smiling at me. I remembered her from that afternoon at the hospital, the day I'd taken Blake's violin to Matt. "Yeah," I mumbled.

"Don't mind him," she said quickly in a low voice. "He's out on pass for the weekend with a miserable case of strep throat, which he never said a word about to the hospital staff. Every little thing — " She fell silent as Matt laboriously turned away from the counter.

He looked at me as I knelt there in front of the baby goods. "So, what are you up to, Sam?" he asked, his voice scratchy.

I cringed. He hadn't called me Sam since my early visits. Was he mad because I hadn't come back to see him? "Working," I said in a hurry. "I come in after school and Saturdays." I crossed my fingers, hoping Mom hadn't heard my half-lie.

"Oh." A strange expression, maybe envy, lingered in his face for a moment. Then he scowled and removed his headset.

I scooted over and put a large tub of Vaseline on the shelf. "What were you listening to?"

"Itzhak Perlman. The batteries are shot and it's dropped a whole tone. It sounds sick below pitch."

I took longer than I needed to straighten the row of small Vaseline containers. "We're working on the Beethoven concerto again," I said, nervous about looking at him. "I heard you're playing it."

Matt glanced at me, then looked at the floor, his mouth set in a bitter line. "Maestro seems to think it'll be a cinch for me to go out there in front of two thousand people."

"Matt, they must sell batteries here," his mother cut in. "Why don't I go look for some."

"I'll find them." His voice was curt.

"They're over there," I said, pointing to the display by the cash register. But Matt had already begun wheeling himself in the opposite direction and didn't see. Humiliated, I sat there on the floor staring at the baby supplies. Then, sensing that Mom was watching me, I methodically put the rest of the stock on the shelf and went back downstairs for more. When I came up again the Bruckners were gone.

Karla came over that evening to spend the night, and I was still out of sorts. Now Deena would be hogging the bedroom and later, the living room. If I had a nightmare and screamed, one more person would find out what a mess I was. Meanwhile, Deena was giggling hysterically as she explained to Karla that Kyle Warren and his friends spent Saturday evenings running across people's roofs, and that he'd promised to yell down our chimney. I ignored the phone when it started ringing, and Deena was too far gone to try to get there in a hurry.

"Sammie?" Mom called. "Phone."

I blinked in surprise. Julie had been out when I'd

tried calling her earlier, and Jen probably was with Tomás.

"I'm sorry I was rude today," Matt said in a still-scratchy voice.

"Well . . . it must be pretty hard. Going places, I mean." Without warning, tears spilled. I held my mouth in a tight knot and tried not to sniffle.

"It's easier to just stay at the hospital." He sounded really down. "Here, I can't even get to my room. It's upstairs."

"How awful." I wiped my eyes on my arm, but tears kept leaking out.

"They're getting a lift put in. They've already built a ramp to the front door."

I forced a smile even though he couldn't see it. "It'll get easier with practice."

"Yeah. That's what they all say."

Deena was peeking around the corner at me. "Can I use the phone?"

I covered the receiver. "Quit bugging me!" I hissed, and turned to face the fridge. I began arranging the ladybug magnets in a line. "Sorry about that."

"Your sister?" he guessed.

"Yeah. She's never satisfied with minding her own business."

There was an awkward pause. Just as I started to blurt out how great it was that he was playing the Beethoven, he said something about batteries. "Sorry," he added, and coughed.

"No prob." And then the back of my neck prickled. The only other person I knew who said that was Julie.

Silence. "I'd better go and study." His voice was flat. "I have a test Monday."

"You mean you have . . ."

"I have school at the hospital. Think I'd want to lose a whole year, besides breaking my back?"

"Well, good luck on your test. And thanks for calling."

He hung up.

Deena chortled when she saw my face. "Sammie's in love."

"I am not!" And then I drew back. Karla was listening, and my voice sounded almost as wild as it did in my dreams.

Mom's arm settled around my shoulder. "Let's just say Sammie is *attuned* to someone."

"Huh?" Deena wrinkled her nose. "What's that supposed to mean?" A moment later feet thundered across our roof and she forgot about me.

Mom gave me a squeeze. "Need to talk?"

I certainly did.

Nineteen

Matt didn't rehearse with Youth Orchestra until our final practice the night before the concert.

It was June. The days were warm and sunny, the air soft and gentle. Baskets of flowers hung from lamp posts. Tourists crowded the streets with their loud colours, cameras and strange accents. A dreamy laziness infected me, making the end of the school year, the concert, my job, all kinds of things, seem unimportant. All I really felt like doing was walking along the water's edge, the sun warm on my back, and looking out over the shining blueness that lay between us and other parts of the world. A lot of people were out. Elderly men and women sat on benches reading newspapers, talking, or simply sitting. Joggers and cyclists sped along the trails while dog walkers meandered from place to place, following the noses of their canine leaders.

I thought about Dad a lot. Once in a while it felt

as if he were with me. When the feeling came, every little act took on a ritualistic importance, rather like when I was younger and had crushes, and wanted to make every move perfect when that boy was around. It was a gentle sort of feeling, and terribly hard to reconcile with the nightmares. They came less often now, but still an underlying fear clutched at me each night. The pages of the notebook filled up, no longer with just the dreams, but with other thoughts of Dad too.

In that sense the concert caught me by surprise.

A nervous anticipation rippled through the air the night of the dress rehearsal. Everybody knew Matt was coming. Julie was doing her cool, collected act, but I knew she was as hyper as a runner at the starting block. So was I. Questions tangled in my mind. How was he? How would he look? Would he want me to come over and say hi? I hadn't seen or talked to him since the day he'd come into the store and then called to apologize, and that was more than a month ago.

Other things worried me, too. The concert hall supposedly was wheelchair-accessible, but the only way to get on stage was to climb seven steps — that, or come through the service entrance where they delivered pianos and bulky stage sets. I knew Maestro had probably worked it all out. I'd seen him pacing with a measuring tape and talking to the stage crew. But still I wondered . . . With Dad all kinds of little things had become formidable obstacles. Things like the width of doorways. Just the smallest curb, or even a bad crack in a sidewalk.

Areas that were too narrow to allow a wheelchair to turn around.

We'd all practised like slaves to get ready for the concert, especially Julie, who learned the entire solo part. I wondered how many hours Matt had spent practising the physical manoeuvres simply to get on and off stage.

Maestro's hair was flapping across his forehead, his gestures bold and dynamic as he conducted us through the end of the *1812 Overture*. As usual he didn't look completely satisfied, but for once he refrained from climbing all over us like a blood-thirsty vulture. "Intermission!" he barked. "The audience will be out fifteen minutes. You have thirteen minutes exactly to break and get back to your places." With brisk strides he swept off.

Most of us sat there as if we were part of the stage set. Matt was probably here, though he might not come onstage until it was time to play. Beside me, Arthur fidgeted with his valve slides. In front of me, Renée swabbed the moisture out of her clarinet. Hilary was leaning forward over her cello, practising a difficult passage. And Julie's right foot tapped impatiently as she studiously ignored Geoff.

Then Amy scooted her chair back and began whispering to Ian in the bassoon section. They sat there, heads together. Amy's long hair gleamed in the bright lights.

Like a sail snapping in a brisk wind, Julie went taut. She looked my way and beckoned. Anger burned in her eyes.

I knew what she was thinking. Several months ago Amy and Ian had become a couple. They had a tendency to glue themselves together in public. Maybe they wouldn't this time, with Matt coming, but I didn't trust Amy. It would be just like her to flaunt her new relationship the very minute Matt wheeled onstage for the first time.

"She better not try anything." Julie spat the words out, not bothering to keep her voice down. "If she does, I'll skewer her personally on my bow."

It was obvious we weren't the only ones thinking along those lines. A muttering arose in the group. Kids got up and started milling around.

I drew in a long breath and grasped the back of a chair. "We could meet him on his way in. You could be talking to him, just in case."

Julie shook her head, eyes uncertain. "I need some air. If I sit here one more minute, they'll have to scrape me off the balcony." I followed her through the wings and out a side door that overlooked the parking lot. She leaned against the metal railing; I sat on the concrete steps.

The sun hung low in the sky. The dull rumble of traffic cut through the cooling air, past the oaks and chestnut trees.

Julie's voice was rough when she spoke next. "You make it sound so easy. 'We could meet him on his way in. You could be talking to him, just in case.' He won't want to speak to me, Sammie. My mother knew exactly what she was doing, and she did it well."

My stomach twisted. I got up and stood there beside her, leaning against the railing. I thought of the times Julie had come to the hospital with no hope. "Maybe he's changed," I said slowly.

"Hah." Julie glanced at her watch. "Time to go. Maestro'll be fuming. I'd just love to puke all over the lovely Amy's lap. That would give her something to think about."

I giggled, then clamped down. Julie was serious. And Matt was probably backstage by now. As we hurried past the enormous ropes that controlled the curtains, I saw a wheelchair making its way through the maze of backstage equipment. Julie slipped away without warning. I wanted to stare, but made my way back to my seat, through the tight formation of chairs and music stands.

Amy and Ian were still whispering, holding hands. Her hair draped across his bassoon. I glared at them, but they were oblivious.

"Some people have a lot of nerve, eh?" Arthur muttered.

"You can say that again." There was no sign of Julie. And from the wings came the sound of wheels rolling. I looked at the music stand I shared with Arthur, then gave it a calculated kick. It careened sideways, clipping Ian on the shoulder. I faked a gasp. "Oh no! I'm sorry." Arthur's yelp was real.

Ian bent over to help us pick up the scattered music. With a scornful look at Arthur and me, Amy slid her chair back into its normal position.

I almost laughed. Arthur grinned, one eye closed in a sly wink.

And then I saw Julie. Coming back onstage, past the cello section, her head was high, her bearing regal. But her face might as well have been carved of ice, her eyes of jade.

Maestro walked briskly to the podium. "Let's get a move on. We need every minute. Principal violin. You enter from the other side. Do it again, and see that the group is in tune." He swept into the wings, followed by Julie with her violin.

The concert hall was deathly still as Julie entered. With the spotlights on us and blackness in the cavernous room, I had no way of knowing if anybody was out there. Julie rehearsed her perfunctory bow to the audience, then directed the oboe to play an A. We tuned. Maestro appeared. Julie sat down. My heart pattered like a frightened animal's. It sped even more rapidly at the sound of wheels, accompanied by a small rhythmic squeak.

Matt appeared, violin in his lap. He was wearing jeans and a designer shirt. His feet, in runners, sat on the metal foot rests. His head was up, his arms strong as he manoeuvred his chair into position.

My breath caught. Somebody started clapping. We all joined in. The sound fell into the huge concert hall like a scattering of leaves. Silence once more. If it were a real concert, the principal violin would rise to shake hands with the soloist. I held my breath, hoping it would work out all right. On cue, Julie stood and extended her hand.

Matt looked at her from his wheelchair. "So you finally got what you wanted, Blaustein," he said.

Her hair gleamed with red and blue lights as she

tossed her head. "I earned it, Bruckner," she retorted. "If you want to forget the solo, I can handle that too."

Shocked whispers rustled through the group. I discovered that my fingernails were biting into the palms of my hands.

Matt's sudden laugh shattered the tension. "I'm sure you can." He paused. "Which cadenza do you play, the Kreisler?"

Julie's mouth gaped, as if in protest. If she spoke, I didn't hear because suddenly kids were mobbing Matt. I lingered in my chair. Would he want to see me? We didn't have any comfortable common ground. Meanwhile Maestro was getting ready to attack his music stand with his baton. "Time's running out!" he snapped.

Maestro worked us mercilessly. Matt's interpretation of the music was different from Julie's. We had to change the tempo in a few spots. My lip began feeling puffy and numb. I wondered how I would've made out if we'd never moved out of the apartment, where I never had a chance to practise. If I'd never bombed that section in the Beethoven symphony; if Maestro had never threatened to kick me out of orchestra. So many things had changed since then.

There was little opportunity to watch Matt — which was exactly what I wanted to do. Or to listen to that glorious violin voice soaring over the rest of our playing. But as I counted out bars of rests, I watched the back of his head, his shoulders, while in the foreground violin bows moved in unison.

It was after ten when we were dismissed. I packed up quickly and headed over to the violin section before I lost my nerve. Matt was drenched with sweat and he looked absolutely beat. His hands trembled as he removed the shoulder rest from his violin. At last he looked up at me.

"It's good to have you back, Matt," I said.

Something flickered in his eyes. "It's good to *be* back." He gave me what looked almost like a smile, then slowly began wheeling his chair toward the wings where a slight, sandy-haired man was waiting, maybe his father.

He was barely moving. My mind flashed back to Dad trying to get somewhere when he was worn out, the way he'd seethe with frustration as he inched along. I wondered if I should offer to help. Then I remembered Matt's reaction to being helped in the pharmacy. He wouldn't want me interfering. I looked over at Julie. For once her face was unguarded. I turned back to Matt. "Want a push?"

He nodded. "That would be great. I had no idea this would be so bloody tiring." His eyes met mine for a moment and I had the sudden feeling that everything I had done was right.

Pushing the wheelchair. It was such a simple act. So normal. The minor obstacles were easy. Past the grand piano. Over an electrical cord. But suddenly I was caught between two worlds. Something heaved in my chest. My eyes burned. "Good show, Matt," I said as I delivered him to the man in the wings. "And good luck tomorrow." For an instant my hand rested on his shoulder.

"Thanks. I'll need it." For an even shorter instant his hand rose and covered mine.

"Sammie, are you okay?" Hilary caught my arm as I wandered back to the formation of chairs.

I managed a smile. "Just kind of choked up."

"I'm glad you helped him. I felt so sorry for him."

Julie joined us. "Sammie's a real pro." The way she said it alluded to far more than merely giving Matt a push. It touched on Dad, on all my hospital visits. But Hilary, of course, only knew about the connection with my father. She smiled and went back to her cello. Julie put her violin away. "Can I come over?" she asked. "Maisie's off, and I need some human company. The old tape recorder just won't do tonight."

I gave her a shaky smile. "Of course, you silly."

"Promise not to scream at 3 a.m.?"

"No. I don't have much control over that unconscious stuff, just ask my sister. Or my mom."

Julie groaned.

The sky still held the last light of sunset as we headed across the parking lot to Julie's Volvo. I looked back at the building and saw a van parked at the service entrance. As I watched, a wheelchair rolled down a ramp connecting the platform and the vehicle. I nudged Julie.

Her face was wistful. "At least he *spoke* to me." She gave me a long, knowing look. "And now *you*, you idiot. Why'd you have to go and fall in love with him too?"

"I — " I broke off, speechless. I couldn't totally

deny it. But it was far more complicated than that, and I knew Julie understood.

"Oh shut up," she said when I didn't speak. "Let's go make popcorn and pig out. I'm scared to death about tomorrow. Matt gets stage fright so bad he pukes every time, and I don't know how he's going to manage that in a tux, in a wheelchair. And if you scream tonight, so will I."

The Fraser Street drawbridge was up. As we waited, darkness filtered over the city, over the water. Up and down the inlet lights reflected in wavery strands. "Hah," Julie said abruptly. "We should hop that barge and get out of this mess. Go someplace exciting, like the Far East."

I adjusted the knobs on her radio. "We'd miss the concert."

"As usual you're right, milady. We'll come back tomorrow."

Stage fright. Worry gnawed at me. Julie and I talked until late, munching popcorn, while overhead, unknown kids jumped from rooftop to rooftop, occasional thumpings in the dark.

Julie looked lovely the night of the concert, cool and serene with diamonds sparkling at her throat and ears. I felt good myself, in my long black dress. Concert night always seemed to transform us, a bunch of kids, into real musicians. In his tux even Arthur looked dashing.

It wasn't just a matter of playing. Beyond the glare of spotlights, a rustling mass of humanity filled the two thousand seats we couldn't really see. I knew Mom and Deena were out there with

Glenna, Greg, Aunt Vivian and Uncle Amos. Jen had said she'd try to make it. Even Mrs. Crosbie had promised to come, if there was space in Greg's car. I knew the Wong family would be there, and Renée's parents too. The Bruckners had front-row seats. For Julie's sake, I hoped Maisie and her father would come. Her mother was still in Paris.

The first half of the concert went without a hitch. In front of us Maestro sculpted the air and we gave him music. It came all around me, the strong vibrant bite of strings, the contrasting voices of brass and woodwinds. The floor trembled beneath my feet. And in the blackness beyond I could feel the audience responding.

Intermission. I was nervous. Everybody was. We dashed to the washroom, paced, not talking much, sat down again. Julie appeared calm, but her tapping right foot gave her away. The crowd filed back to their places.

Maestro stood to face the audience. "As many of you know, one of our members suffered a tragic accident last fall." His voice went out, a frail human connection across the vast space. I heard stirrings, then the silence of absolute attention. "It means more than I can possibly say to welcome Matt Bruckner back for one final concert. It's our loss that he won't be with us next year, but ultimately we shall all gain. Matt has been granted early admission to the University of Toronto, where he will be receiving a full scholarship to continue his study of the violin. Please join me in welcoming a truly courageous and talented musician, Matthew Aaron Bruckner."

Matt — *leaving?* As uproarious applause shook the concert hall, I looked at Julie. Her mouth was slack. But Matt was already wheeling onto the stage. His face was white. He looked positively ill in the blinding glare of the lights. *Matt*, I wanted to say. *We're all with you. You'll do fine.* Without fully realizing what I was doing, I stood up, clapping. Then Julie was on her feet, and Geoff Harris-Hughes too. Hilary. Renée. Even Amy. The standing ovation went on and on. As Matt glanced around, caught between the audience and us, I saw unexpected moisture shining in his eyes, on his cheeks.

After the concert I read a review of it in the paper. The writer couldn't seem to find enough good things to say about the Beethoven; he went on and on about Matt's incredible performance. At the time, sitting in the middle of the orchestra it was like nothing I'd ever experienced before. Somehow I was no longer Samantha Franklin, but instead, part of this *entity*, a oneness that was our group, and more. The music surged through us, around us, and it didn't seem of our own making. Matt's violin sang like a human voice, crying out the sorrows and joys of all humankind. It bonded us, guided us, soared high above us searching toward the farthest reaches of existence. I cried when he played the tender, serene middle movement. But I no longer needed to see the music, only the white tracings of Maestro's baton.

When it ended there was first a stunned stillness. Then the entire hall erupted. Stamping. Cheering. Whistles. Shouts. Matt shook hands with Maestro. He shook hands with Julie, then kissed her fingers. I was positive his face was wet with tears, but my own eyes were so blurry I couldn't be sure.

The audience wouldn't let him rest. Over the cries of "Bravo! Bravo!" exploded new calls for "More! More!" The applause fell into a thundering rhythmic beat that shook the floor and walls, and was silenced only when Matt lifted his violin to his shoulder once more. A collective sigh hushed throughout as he began a slow Bach movement for solo violin. This time I could listen with my full attention. Tingles ran along my nerves. My scalp prickled. The music held a mystical power, opening me, thrusting aside all other awareness.

It was a generous but ravenous audience. The ovation was overwhelming. But they continued to want more. After the Bach even I could see, from my distance, that Matt was worn with fatigue, trembling and scarcely able to hold his violin.

As if it had been planned that way all along, Julie stood up and grasped the handles of his wheelchair. As the tumultuous applause continued, she gracefully ushered Matt offstage.

Twenty

Summer and my seventeenth birthday came and went. It was a strange patchwork of events that centred more around my job than anything else. Roger hired me half-time once school was out. My position included some cashier work, for Mom had been promoted to pharmacist's assistant and was now helping with the prescriptions. After my first heady experiences learning to use the cash register, I decided that dealing with invoices and pricing was more interesting than waiting on customers. But the extra money made a big difference.

So while Julie was whisked off to places with exotic names, I worked, practised a lot and spent some time with Jennifer now and then. And daydreamed. Matt was constantly on my mind. Although Julie hadn't been quite on target when she put a name to my feelings, she'd come close. I couldn't honestly say I was *in love* with Matt

Bruckner, not in the usual way, but feelings were there and they were strong. I found myself watching for wheelchairs, though Port Salish was so large that chances of seeing him were slim. Besides, Julie really cared about him. And he was going away.

I tried to push it all back. Mrs. Crosbie introduced me to Mr. Kirkpatrick, who'd known Dad's family. He was a willowy old gentleman who wore a green feather tucked in the band of his grey tweed hat. One day he walked over to show me the house, cane in one hand, pipe in the other.

"They were a lively family," he said past the stem of his pipe, puffing curls of aromatic smoke around us. "Several boys; most of them joined the navy, as I recall. Billy, I think, did not." He stopped to pet an Irish setter on a leash. "Good morning, Mrs. Griffith," he said to the dog's owner. "Fine day, is it not?" The old man and I walked on at a leisurely pace, admiring roses in full bloom and lovely rock gardens with heather and larkspur. "The last I heard of young Billy was that he'd hitch-hiked down to San Francisco on his way to see the world. I never knew he settled back in these parts."

Everything around me stilled as if the whole world were poised, motionless, before a wide-angle lens. Dad's San Francisco days, his hippie time. He'd never spoken much about that part of his life, only that that was where he'd met Glenna's mother, and they'd come back here before Glenna was born because they didn't like the Vietnam War and wanted their child to be born Canadian.

It was mind-boggling to think of Dad being my age and, like Julie, wanting to break free.

"This is where they lived," Mr. Kirkpatrick continued as we rounded a corner. He indicated a small green house tucked neatly back in a narrow lot behind a white picket fence. "They were here a good number of years, but after the kids left, Ed and Thelma packed up too."

"They're in Florida," I said. "In a retirement centre." We rarely heard from Grandpa and Grandma Franklin these days; I guessed they were happy with their lives just the way they were.

"Well, is that so." Mr. Kirkpatrick thoughtfully stroked his chin. "Seems you can never guess what will come of folks."

I thanked him for his trouble and stood there a while in the glorious sunlight after he'd walked on. The little green house. I tried to imagine it full of boys, boys vaulting over the picket fence, crushing the daisies. I tried to imagine Dad bursting out that front door, letting it slam behind him. It was just a small ordinary house. In fact, it was on the bus route and I'd been past it hundreds of times. I wondered if Mom knew.

* * *

Matt phoned me when Julie was in Greece. "Are you doing anything right now?" he asked.

It was my day off and I'd been sitting on the back steps watching butterflies flitting around the morning glories, wishing I weren't so cut off from my old friends at school and wondering if I should take a walk along the beach. "No," I said.

"I'm growing mould, I'm so bored sitting around the house. Want to go do something?"

The invitation caught me so much by surprise that I nearly dropped the phone. "Sure. I can't drive yet," I added, not wanting to admit that we still didn't have a car.

Matt muttered something, and an image of the public transit vehicles for the disabled popped into my mind. Dad had used them occasionally to come home when he got a pass. "What about the Handi-Van?" I said. "I could meet you somewhere."

There was a startled silence. "All right." A spark ignited in Matt's voice. "My mom's not here. I'll bet she takes a fit when she comes home and finds a note."

I laughed. It was preposterous for a guy Matt's age to talk about leaving notes for his mother — except something told me this was the first time he'd needed to do it since his accident. "Where should I meet you?"

He hesitated. "The fountain at Civic Square? Do you think I could get around that part of town?"

I was stung by the uncertainty in his voice. A year ago he'd had access to any place he wanted to go. "Sure. Anyhow, I'll be there if you get stuck. What time?"

"Race you. Let's see who gets there first."

I did, slow as the bus system was. Sitting on a bench soaking in sunlight and traffic sounds, I tossed crumbs to the chortling pigeons that occupied the square. The fountain spurted and splashed, marking off time. Fifteen minutes passed and I began wondering if he'd changed his mind. Or if maybe it was all a joke. Then a small white bus, marked with green and blue, pulled over.

I felt so fluttery I drew in a deep breath. "Stop it, Sammie," I muttered. "He only called because he was bored." Nevertheless, I checked my top, my shorts, my sandals, to make sure I was presentable. The van doors opened. With a whine, the small elevator lowered itself to street level. Matt removed his Walkman headset and rolled off in his chair.

He was actually grinning. "I can't believe I did this."

His mood was contagious. "Next thing you know, you'll be premiering at Carnegie Hall. Or running for Parliament."

Matt shook his head. "I'd better get used to it, with Toronto coming up." The sun was bright on his reddish hair, though his skin was still pale compared to the hundreds of passersby.

I tossed more bread crumbs to the pigeons, then handed Matt the bag. The birds crowded around. He scattered food nearby and put a hunk the size of a marble on the arm of his chair. An aggressive bird with an iridescent sheen to its feathers cocked its head first one way then the other, and fluttered up to light on the chair. Matt laughed out loud as the pigeon snatched at the prize, only to drop it onto the head of one of the birds below. Muttering at the explosive sound, the pigeons flowed away like a fleet of sailboards in a stiff breeze.

"So what do you want to do?" I asked.

Matt gave me a funny half-smile. "Just be here. It's been almost a year, you know." He wheeled over to the fountain and tried to put his hand in the water. He couldn't reach. A pang shot through me. He yanked the armrest off his chair. Holding tightly to the other one, he leaned sideways and dabbled his fingers in the pool. Without warning, water splashed over me.

"Oh!" I jumped backwards to sit on the rim of the pool.

Matt leaned back, grinning. "Got you."

"Typical male power play," I teased, swishing my hands in the water. "Have to show you control the environment." Then I tensed as Matt's face went blank. It was one of Julie's favourite comebacks.

"Did Julie Blaustein put you up to all those visits?" he demanded in a tight voice, after a deafening silence.

My mouth went dry. "No. The first time, Amy made us come. After that I just . . . went." Except once. Heat roared into my face. I looked into the greeny water of the fountain where pennies, nickels and dimes lay scattered across the bottom.

Matt was quiet a long time. At last he jammed the armrest back into the frame of his wheelchair. "I'm not a pawn in a chess game." His voice was rough. He turned his back on me.

My legs were trapped between the fountain and

the wheelchair. Indignation burned in me as I slid sideways, trying to get free. After all that worrying. After everything — how could he be so cynical?

He moved the chair for me.

I fled to a bench nearby, where I kicked at a melting orange popsicle that lay near my feet.

"Sammie."

I wouldn't look at him.

"Sammie. I'm sorry. I've had too much time to think about things."

"Everybody was so worried about you," I muttered. "Really worried. You can't blame people for that."

He looked away and rubbed one hand across the back of his neck. "I said I'm sorry." He wheeled his chair backwards a bit, then forwards, then back again in a pacing pattern. I watched as he squished the remains of the popsicle, but said nothing.

Tourists and city-dwellers ambled past, laughing, talking, dangling shopping bags. I felt anonymous in the midst of so many strangers, and was glad of it. I tucked my feet beneath me on the bench. The pigeons were clustering around some girls about Deena's age, who were throwing popcorn. I looked everywhere except at Matt. Up the flagpoles. At the sea gulls screeching overhead.

At last he spoke. "Have you gotten over your dad?"

I tapped my fingers on the warm bench. "Not really. I still dream about him."

Matt's face shadowed. He seemed to shudder.

"You too?" It made sense. In a way I was relieved.

Matt shifted in his chair. "The other night I yelled so loud my parents thought I was being stabbed or something."

"Join the club," I said.

He swore and turned to watch a kid who was skateboarding. The boy swept right past Matt's wheelchair as if Matt weren't even there. I winced and looked at Matt's legs that could no longer move, and wondered if he'd ever used a skateboard.

"Let's wal — Let's see what's happening over there," Matt said abruptly, gesturing toward a group of street musicians.

"Sure." I kept my voice nonchalant, pretending I hadn't noticed his slip.

As we approached, the music became clearly audible, a rollicking Irish tune. My feet wanted to skip along to the beat. Craftspeople were selling handmade jewellery and wooden toys nearby. Two mime artists, their faces painted black and white, went through a routine. The musicians were long-haired and relaxed, and the music seemed to pour out effortlessly. I stood there, feet tapping, and lost myself.

A burst of applause startled me. I joined in, clapping until my palms stung. Matt was struggling for something in his pocket; then he tossed a loonie into an open violin case. "Let's go," he said.

I wanted to stay, but Matt seemed incredibly restless. So we hung around downtown and wandered from place to place. Sometimes Matt's face would light up and he'd sit there soaking in the surroundings; later he'd close himself off and be in a hurry to get someplace else. It was a strange couple of hours because he didn't talk very much. Twice he got himself stuck, but managed to get out of it without my help. When we went our separate ways I was almost relieved.

In spite of the time we'd spent together, I realized in many ways I hardly knew Matt Bruckner. He was easier to talk to on the phone.

* * *

The end of August came. Matt was leaving for Toronto.

Julie evaded her mother's plans for some major shopping that day and picked me up at the house. We wandered into the airport an hour before Matt's flight and found him at a check-in line. His parents stood with him, amidst a mountain of suitcases and boxes. "They'll stay a while to help him settle in," Julie said in my ear. Then she planted herself directly in front of Matt. "So, Bruckner. You're running out on us."

Matt looked first at her, then at me. His face was burnished with sun and new freckles; his eyes were clear. "I know you too well for that, Blaustein," he retorted with a half-smile.

"Why don't you kids get something to eat," Matt's father cut in, handing Matt a ten dollar bill. "There's no point in all of us waiting in line."

Matt rolled his chair along briskly, with Julie and me on either side.

"How does it feel? To be on your way, I mean."

Matt shot me a quizzical glance. "Good. Terrifying."

It would be terrifying. I gave him an embarrassed smile, keenly aware of the gap that lay between us.

The loudspeaker cut into my thoughts, but the crowds of moving people were a vivid reminder that Matt's leaving marked yet another departure in my life. Like it or not, a major part of the past year had been focused on him, and now I'd be left with another blank space.

Julie and Matt were talking in clipped sentences that on the surface seemed to mean very little, but that obviously went deeper. I fell behind, not wanting to intrude. And then Maestro appeared just as we were entering the Snack Shoppe. The four of us gathered around a table. Matt's wheelchair blocked most of the aisle. And we had the kind of stilted conversation that happens when people who aren't relaxed sit down and try to talk to one another.

The time went too quickly. "I'll go wait at your car," I told Julie as we joined Matt's parents just outside the security entrance.

"Hang on a sec." She looked vulnerable.

Maestro was saying goodbye to Matt. I wondered whose turn would be next, Julie's or mine. Mine, obviously, for Julie hung back. I stood before him, not knowing what to say. Matt's brown eyes were warm, but they held a trace of impatience, as well. "I hope everything works out," I said in a rush, then cowered. It sounded so dumb — except, I meant it. Totally.

He gave me his funny half-smile, one hand raised almost in a salute. I mirrored his action and somehow we ended up in a hug. "You're a good kid, Sammie," he said, and let me go.

I turned and walked away so I wouldn't see Julie's farewell. Swift footsteps caught up with me. Matt's mother touched my arm and looked into my face for a long moment.

"Matt may not realize this just yet," she said at last, "but it's something any mother would know." She broke off, gazing at me with eyes that were so like Matt's. "I thought I was going to lose both of them." Her voice went tremulous. "You helped bring back my son, Sammie. That's a gift no mother could ever repay."

I just looked at her, unable to speak.

She accepted my silence, smiling now. "Bless you, Sammie. You'll always have a special place in my heart." She squeezed my hand and was gone.

Julie caught up with me on the down escalator. In a seemingly casual gesture she draped her arm around my shoulder. I returned the favour and our heads bumped together in a sisterly way. We went out to the parking lot.

She stopped along a roadside near the airport, where we watched the roaring jet thrust into the sky. It dwindled to a silver glint trailing a plume of exhaust, then vanished into the blue. There was a knot in my throat that lasted a long time.

"I know what we should do," Julie said, subdued, after a whole procession of jets had come and gone. She turned the key in the ignition and raced with tight control along the curving roads. We drove by the water's edge, through densely forested areas, but always staying far from the city. Finally she parked at the ferry terminal. We got out, walked on board. We spent the rest of that day riding back and forth between Stewart's Bay and Wainwright. The sun was warm on the promenade deck, the salt breeze clean as it whipped the hair back from our faces. We stood there watching the water slice into frothy green-white turbulence, watching the greedy sea gulls circle, screaming for food. And in Parsons Pass, where the boat seemed to tilt and the horn gave an extra blast, where the shores of the islands were dotted with what looked to be toy houses, churches and docks, we watched eagles soaring overhead.

Twenty-one

*S*chool started. Orchestra started. Surprise of surprises, with Troy and Jason graduated and gone, my audition earned me the position of principal horn, with good old Arthur beside me in second chair. Surprise again, Arthur started asking me out — nothing glamorous, just the odd show or skating, but it was fun in a companionable kind of way.

"Have you heard from Matt?" I asked Julie as she drove me home after practice one day.

Her lips curved in an enigmatic smile. "A letter now and then. His teacher is fabulous. Classes are okay. I have a feeling the wheelchair part is pretty hard. Mostly it's what he *doesn't* say. He's in an apartment with three other guys, one's a paid attendant for him." She winced. "You know what lots of people must think — needing a guy to help him in and out of the bathtub, and all that." She shook her head. Anger snapped from the loose ends of her hair. "Little do they know." She honked at a taxi that changed lanes without signalling. "Sammie," she said, "that kid is one of a kind."

I nodded but didn't speak. I couldn't, just then.

I had another one of my dreams that night. Dad and I were in the living room of the little green house. Sunlight poured through the windows. We were happy. But then a savage gust of wind slammed against the house, shattering the glass panes and sweeping Dad high up against the ceiling. "It's all right, Sammie," he said. "Don't be frightened." I picked up a large shard of glass, looked through it. Now it was Matt up by the ceiling, and Dad was just a picture on the wall. I looked frantically at the clock and the numbers began falling off, one by one. I tried to call out, reaching for Dad, reaching for Matt, but no matter how hard I tried, they were always just beyond my grasp. I hurled the glass out the window, out into the roaring wind. Another blast; the house blew away in scatterings of lumber and roof tiles. Again I tried to call out — yet there was comfort nearby.

I awakened trembling, my throat dry. Deena was still snoring, so probably I hadn't screamed this time. Cuddled against my cheek was Dominic, a purring, friendly ball. I stroked him; he gave a sleepy "Mrrt?" and stretched, then shoved against me in an affectionate way. I lay awake for a long time.

The next day was one of my work days. It was a slow afternoon. At the last minute Mom had to fill an order for all kinds of chemicals for some kid's science experiment. Caustic ammonia smells wafted through the pharmacy, then the sharp bite of acid. Just before we got off work, Mom poured some ether. The keen odour penetrated right into me, making me feel a little woozy.

"*Air!*" Mom gasped as we stepped outside. "That stuff makes me sick. They used ether to put me out for my tonsillectomy when I was seven. It's an experience you never forget."

I tossed my backpack over my shoulder. "Do you like your job, Mom?"

She looked at me a moment as we waited at the bus stop. "Yes, actually. It's a lot different from teaching, but the management is kind, as you know, and it's far more interesting now that I'm away from that silly cash register."

"You're more like *you* again." I leaned toward the street to see if the bus was coming. It was.

Mom laughed. "Good. I'm beginning to feel that way. Life certainly hasn't turned out to be what I expected, but I can't complain."

We found seats together, a miracle during rush hour. As the bus noisily jerked and braked along the city streets, I gazed out the window. It was a soft grey day, with outlines blurring a bit in the distance. Yet up close, vivid October colour blazed like sunlight, the golds of trees, and the rich crimson of ivy as it sprawled across fences and the walls of older buildings. We went past the wharf, where hundreds of bare masts probed the sky, and then past the old Franklin house.

"That was a long time ago, wasn't it, Sammie," Mom murmured.

I fingered my French horn necklace that she'd given me for Christmas. "Yeah."

"I think it's time we looked into private lessons for you again," Mom said as we got off the bus.

My feet struck the pavement. "We can't afford it, Mom. You know that."

"Our house will be paid off in four years," Mom said drily. "And believe me, lessons are far cheaper than counselling. Most of your friends in orchestra take lessons, don't they?"

"Well, yeah . . ." My years of music lessons seemed so long ago. They'd stopped about the time Dad got sick for the last time. I swallowed hard. "It's still expensive. Who says I can't teach myself?"

"Seriously, Sammie." Mom was looking intently at me. "You have a lot of talent. It's a shame to let it go to waste."

I tried some evasive action. "Julie says I ought to get hold of the Mozart horn concertos and learn them. You don't have to be taking private lessons to play in solo festival. And that's not until next spring. There's lots of time to get ready."

"Hmmm."

We were home. Mom unlocked, hung her coat in the closet.

Deena bounded in. "At last. You're home." She dumped a garbage bag full of small packets onto the coffee table.

"What's all this?" Mom asked. "Deena, aren't these supposed to be delivered with your flyers?"

Deena stamped her foot. She was blushing. "Mom! How can I give these to people like Mrs. Crosbie and Mr. O'Reilly? They're gonna think I'm a pervert."

I went closer. And then I started to laugh. There on the coffee table were dozens of samples of a new kind of mini pad. "Total absorption," the package said.

"Do I *have* to?" Deena wheedled. "Mr. O'Reilly sure isn't going to be thrilled and go out and buy more. At least we'll use them. I'll be delivering them — just not to every house on my route."

Mom sat down and laughed harder than I'd seen her laugh in a long time. "All right, Deena, you decide for yourself."

My sister grabbed a banana and headed out the door. "I'm going over to Lisa's. See you later." The door banged shut, then opened again. "Oh, Sammie, a package came for you. It's in the kitchen."

Surprised, I went to get it. The parcel wasn't very big, and it was soft when I picked it up. The handwriting was unfamiliar. When I looked at the return address, my knees went weak. M. Bruckner. On Lowther Avenue, in Toronto. My hands fumbled with the wrapping.

It was a small Scotty dog, a black one. Holding a French horn.

Tears filled my eyes.

It was only then that I noticed the square of paper still tucked in with the brown wrapping. My hands shook as I opened it.

20 October, 1992

Dear Sammie,

Today it's exactly one year since the accident.

This is a hard letter to write. Here I am in T.O., things going as well as can be expected. Some things are good, others not so great. Music here is the greatest.

But this letter isn't about me. I might never have made it here. I might never have made it anywhere.

I've been thinking about you lately. I never really got to know you. At first I didn't care. Later I was scared, I guess. But you were a friend just the same.

Thanks, Sammie. Thanks for everything.

Keep making music,
Matt

"Is it anything interesting, Sammie?" Mom wandered into the kitchen.

I showed her the dog, held out the letter.

"That was very thoughtful of him," she said after a moment. Her arm came around me.

We went back to the living room, sat on the couch. I cuddled the little dog until Dominic pounced out of somewhere and started batting at it. "Hey, you! That's mine!"

Mom laughed. "He just wants to get in on a good thing." Then she cleared her throat. "Sammie, I found something — and I assure you I wasn't snooping; I just wondered what a notebook was doing under the piano."

It didn't bother me that she'd found it. "I felt like writing some things down," I mumbled.

"That was a good idea." Mom hesitated. "It's been a difficult time for you, Sammie. You've had to carry far too much on your shoulders. You've grown up a lot."

I stretched impatiently. I wasn't in the mood for a lecture, not even a friendly one. What I really wanted to do was sprawl on my bed. Read Matt's letter a hundred times, hold the dog against my cheek. Cry. And phone Julie, eventually.

Mom noticed my restlessness. She smiled. "I'll get supper started. I'd like to talk to you some more this evening. Preferably when Deena's tied up on the phone — or with luck, doing her homework."

"Sure," I said, and got up.

A few hours later, with the steady chatter of Deena's voice in the background, I found Mom in the living room. "You wanted to talk to me?"

She smiled and pulled something out from beneath the Sears catalogue. "I'd intended to save this for Christmas, Sammie, but now seems like it might be a better time." She handed me a photo album. "After I found your journal I couldn't resist sampling a few entries here and there. This has the same general idea."

I opened it. It was filled with pictures of Dad. Of Dad and me, doing things together, starting when

I was a baby up until my teens. On the last page was a photo I'd never seen.

A man in a wheelchair was looking out a window. The picture was taken from behind, but there was no question about the identity of the two people in it. I was sitting on a chair arm next to my father. My arm was around his shoulder. We were both looking out the window, into the sunlight.

"Oh *Mom*!" I whispered, overcome.

"That was the last picture ever taken of him," she said quietly. "I wasn't sure when would be the best time to give it to you, but now I think you're ready."

Printed in Canada